HIDER/SEEKER

OTHER BOOKS BY JEN CURRIN

The Sleep of Four Cities
Hagiography
The Inquisition Yours
School

HIDER/SEEKER

Stories

JEN CURRIN

ANVIL PRESS / VANCOUVER

This is a work of fiction. Names, characters, business, events and incidents
are the products of the author's imagination. Any resemblance to actual
persons, living or dead, or actual events is purely coincidental.

Anvil Press Publishers Inc.
P.O. Box 3008, Main Post Office
Vancouver, B.C. V6B 3X5 CANADA
www.anvilpress.com

Library and Archives Canada Cataloguing in Publication

Currin, Jen, author
Hider/seeker / Jen Currin. – First edition.

Short stories.
ISBN 978-1-77214-117-7 (softcover)

I. Title.

PS8605.U77H53 2018   C813'.6   C2018-901822-4

Printed and bound in Canada
Cover design by Rayola Graphic Design
Cover painting by Rebecca Chaperon
Interior by HeimatHouse
Represented in Canada by Publishers Group Canada
Distributed by Raincoast Books

The publisher gratefully acknowledges the financial assistance of the Canada
Council for the Arts, the Canada Book Fund, and the Province of British
Columbia through the B.C. Arts Council and the Book Publishing Tax Credit.

for my beloved communities

TABLE OF CONTENTS

The Charlatan   9

Up the Mountain   13

Seize   37

The Adventure   49

The Garden of Vows   53

Girlfriend/Boyfriend   69

Dinner Party   79

The Shape   87

After Halloween   93

Hide and Seek   95

Midnight   107

The Magician   109

The Rash   117

Insomnia   125

Third Beach   129

The Sisters and the Ash   139

The Fox   143

A Snake in the Grass   161

Seeker   177

Hider   191

Acknowledgments

About the Author

THE CHARLATAN

We were in Canada, but that didn't mean anything.

At the next table I heard them telling stories. "Fucking faggot." "Fag couldn't even throw the ball." Raucous laughter. They must have said the word five, seven times.

I kissed my girlfriend on the mouth and headed to the gender inclusive washroom. As hot air blasted my hands dry, I thought about saying something to them. I decided not to.

Then I was standing in front of their table. Two young women with half-shaved heads and piercings sipped pints of amber beer. A bearded dude in a trucker cap emblazoned with "East Van Baseball League" had his arm around one of them. They looked like any other East Van hipsters, looked like they'd have fairly decent politics. Closest to me, a guy with stringy long hair attacked his steak with a fork and knife. Across from him, a brawny man with a shaved head devoured a hamburger. They were all talking loudly, but I recognized two of the voices—they belonged to the two men closest to me.

9

"Excuse me," I said. "I was just sitting at the next table with my girlfriend, and we couldn't help but overhear...I mean...I heard some language..." I was stumbling. "I mean, do any of you identify as queer?" It came out more awkwardly than I hoped. But then, I had not intended to have this conversation.

I looked around the table. The two women looked stricken or stunned—I wasn't sure which. No one spoke, and then the bald man looked at me with bloodshot eyes. "Fuck off," he said loudly. "Fuck off and leave me alone. I'm trying to eat my dinner." He lifted his hamburger. Grease from the burger ran down his hands.

His stringy-haired companion chimed in, "We were just talking about our friend. He can't throw. It didn't mean anything." He was wearing a "Make America Great Again" tee shirt, which I had originally thought was ironic. Now I wasn't so sure.

"It's just—I'm queer," I said. "And it's really jarring to sit here and hear that kind of language—"

"Fuck off," the bald man said again. "I'm trying to eat my dinner. I don't care. Leave me alone."

The place was called The Charlatan. It was one, I guess. Posing as a cool cafe on a street of freethinkers, artists, and queers. But also home to people like this.

"It's a free country," Stringy continued, still clutching knife and fork as he itched his chin with his wrist. "We were just talking about our friend. It's a free country. We can say what we want."

The trucker cap guy and the two hipster women hadn't said a thing. I couldn't tell if they were mortified or indifferent. Behind me, my girlfriend hovered. She had her hand on my elbow as if she was prepared to yank me out the door if it got more violent.

"I hear you," I said to Stringy. "But the thing is, I'm sitting right next to you. And we're sharing this space. So it's public space. And just as I wouldn't use language that would offend you, I would hope—"

"Leave us alone," the bald one barked. He had set down his dripping burger and clutched his pint in his meaty hand. "Just fuck off. We don't care."

And that was it—my girlfriend tugged at my arm and we were outside in the wind with the swirling leaves, the baggy-panted Rastas talking on the corner, the warrior-mothers pushing strollers. We walked past cafes where green-haired queers hunched over laptops and old Portuguese men sipped espressos in corners crammed with fake marble statues. We were still in Canada, I reminded myself, digging my hands deep into my coat pockets. My girlfriend wrapped her arm around my shoulder and kissed my cold cheek. As we walked I tried to look at each stranger's face as if I knew them.

UP THE MOUNTAIN

The bus shudders to a halt. "Someone wanted the monastery?" the driver calls out. I grab my backpack and stumble to the front. The driver points to a small, painted wooden sign at the side of the road.

After an hour on a muddy path, I reach a wooden arch painted in faded tones of orange and burgundy. The words "Kanda Monastery" are barely visible underneath a tangle of tattered prayer flags. In the distance I hear something that sounds like laughter, then something that sounds like two stones crashing together. I stop to listen. Firs and pines tower overhead. Two birds chatter; a clacking crow interrupts them, swooping down. My face is bathed in sweat, but I am cold under my damp clothes and very thirsty. I am an amateur binder and have wrapped the ACE bandage too tightly—it feels like it is binding my lungs. I wish I had inherited a flatter chest from my father's side of the family, but my mother's Ukrainian genes have endowed me with a stocky frame and these ridiculous breasts.

I adjust my pack and walk under the arch. As I do, the air seems to lighten, grow warmer. I turn a corner and see it: a large wooden building with majestic sloping eaves, several meditation huts trailing out toward the woods behind it. Light streams down from the sun breaking free from the clouds.

In front of the building, a chubby man lies on a small patch of grass, his worn saffron robe pulled up, exposing short brown legs to the sun. I am unsure whether I should approach him or wait for him to notice me, so I linger at the edge of the grass.

Finally he opens his eyes. Seeing me, he quickly sits up and dusts off his legs, then pulls down his robe. Still sitting, he offers me his hand. I'm not sure if I'm supposed to shake it or help him up.

"Mikio?" he asks.

"That's me," I say, deepening my voice.

He smiles as he shakes my hand, looking into my eyes. His face is open, amused, and surprisingly unlined, as he is not young. "I am Somchai. Some call me Ajahn Somchai or just Ajahn. But call me Som if you like."

Surprised by his informality, I simply nod.

"You already took off your hair, I see." He points at my head.

"I thought I was supposed to." I don't tell him that I have been shaving my head for years.

"It's good, it's good!" He smiles. "You are prepared." He gestures to a cleared space to the right of the hall where two young white men hold rocks in their hands and discuss something. They are both skinny, with shaved heads, one tall and one short, in matching saffron robes.

"What are they doing?" I ask.

Somchai smiles. "Building a labyrinth." He hoists himself to his feet. "Come."

As we get closer, I can see that the young monks have already placed some rocks in a large circle and are starting on the second ring. The taller one is holding a large chunk of granite that looks too heavy for the strength of his thin fingers. The shorter one is crouched down, scrubbing a rock with a toothbrush. Next to his feet are a rag and a pail of water.

"Here is Mikio," Somchai says as he approaches. "I told you. He will be staying with us for a while. Mikio, this is John and this, Rolf." He points at each.

The monks look at me shyly and smile. "Welcome," John, the tall one, says, setting down the rock and extending his hand. Do I imagine it, or is there a question in his eyes as he stares into mine? I wish I had a moustache, a beard to cover my face. But of course I would have to shave it here anyway. John does not lower his eyes to my chest, but I am nervous the binding might have slipped. I shake his hand and glance down at the short one bent over his task. He doesn't rise to greet me, but this doesn't seem strange or rude. I notice that he has a heart shaved in the back of his head.

Somchai looks at them tenderly. "They are working very hard," he says to me as we walk toward the large building.

Just this morning I woke up in the city and met up with my friend Stacey, who, after two cups of coffee and a cigarette, gave me an important lesson. "Wrap it like this," she had instructed, pulling the bandage taut around my chest. She made it look so easy—but then, she had been binding since she was a teenager. I thought I understood her instructions, but I must have done something wrong, because the bandage still pinches under my arms.

"You won't feel a thing," Stacey had said. "Except free. No one staring at your tits. It feels great."

"You never wanted them off?" I asked, pointing at her breasts.

She looked at me, shocked. "No. I like them. I just don't want to share them with everyone."

Other friends had theirs removed. They spoke of how liberating it was. "I'll never wear a jogging bra again," my friend Lewis had crowed.

That evening we all meditate together for the first time. There are only six of us—the two white boys; Tep and Suchart, two monks from Thailand; Somchai; and me. Somchai sits at the front on a purple mat, eyes closed, a bell on the floor beside him. Everyone settles onto their cushions, crossing their legs. I lift my shoulders up and pull them back, relaxing them as they lower. The silence has a tangible quality. I take it like air into my lungs. I can breathe better now that I have rewrapped the bandage. Birds trill outside and a robe rustles as someone shifts. Moments tick by, although there is no clock to measure them. It seems we are waiting, but I'm not sure for what. Is this meditation?

After some time, Somchai opens his eyes. "Tonight I will talk about my teacher." An almost-sigh escapes the mouths of a couple of the monks. "Some of you have heard stories," Somchai continues, as if he has read their minds. "But there is still a lot you don't know. A lot to learn from." He reaches under his mat and pulls out a tattered photo, holding it in his lap and looking at it lovingly. Then he leans forward and passes it to Tep in the first row. Tep studies it for a while, and then passes it to Suchart. Finally, it makes its way to me. I hold the picture carefully. It shows an old shaved-headed woman in red robes sitting in front of a stand of bamboo, beaming.

"My mother," Somchai says, nodding at me and the monks.

"One day—" Somchai glances at his arm and carefully removes an ant from his sleeve, lowering it to the floor. "—One day, after my sister and I went to school, my mother said to my father, 'I'm going to Buddha now.' That was all. He did not stop her. She went to live at the monastery. But—" he pauses and shakes his head sadly, "they didn't ordain her."

I pass the picture back to John, who is sitting in front of me.

"Why?" Somchai asks. "Because she was a woman. Finally, she had to go to Sri Lanka. And then she came back and started her monastery."

John glances at the photo before handing it to Rolf, who sits next to him. Rolf holds it carefully for a moment, then gives it back to Suchart.

"Some of you know, I trained with Venerable Ajahn Sun. He lived in cobra and tiger jungles, in caves, hungry, alone in the rain. He taught many things. But my mother, my mother..." He trails off, grasping the photo, which has made its way back into his hand. Then he carefully tucks it back under his mat and looks at each of our faces. "Any questions?"

There is an expectant silence, punctuated by the creaks and rustles of the monks shifting on their mats. Finally John breaks it. "My practice...my practice," he begins quietly. "I mean...I've been struggling with my practice."

Somchai nods for him to continue.

"My mind. It just won't...I can't stop thinking—"

Somchai makes a cutting gesture with his arm and John immediately stops talking. Somchai picks up the bell and rings it. "Bells ring. Minds think. Just follow the breath, pay attention. Don't take thoughts so seriously." He pauses and looks around at us again. "Any more?"

I want to ask how long I should meditate in my hut, how I will know if I am really meditating, but I don't want to appear foolish.

When no one replies, Somchai smiles. "Then rest. Take rest."

Somchai has assigned me the hut farthest away from the meditation hall—it is almost in the woods. I forgot to bring a flashlight, and can barely see the path in the light of the half-moon, so step cautiously, hoping I don't crush any living thing. I hear the monks shuffling off to their huts in the darkness. None of them have flashlights either.

Bundled up in my sleeping bag and a hat to keep my ears warm, I can't sleep. The room is tiny, already full of my breath—claustrophobic. Hours pass. It is very dark. The tall trees scrape the windows and I hear rustling outside, the hoot of an owl. The glass of the window is thin, the door flimsy—a bear could easily break through it. But I am not afraid of animals, really, or of nature. It's ghosts I am worried about.

I turn over on my stomach and pull the sleeping bag over my head. I hum tunelessly to comfort myself. And then I feel it.

It's—a presence. No other way to describe it. There's a presence in the room. It appears in one of the corners by the door and comes closer. Fear radiates from the pit of my stomach. I feel it crouching down next to the foot of my mat. Shaking, I bury my face deeper into the sleeping bag.

"Not at night," I say in my mind. "I told you not to come at night."

The presence pulses an answer: "Where are you during the day?"

He has a point. Since his death, I have rushed through my days like someone trying to put out a fire—from work to the gym, to the bar with friends, back to my apartment after midnight to fall into bed and the blessed annihilation of sleep. But here, in the quiet and solitude of the forest, he has found me.

"I wish I'd been able to say goodbye." I still can't bring myself to lift my head out of the sleeping bag.

"Everyone feels that way. I had to go quickly."

"Why?"

"I was needed at home."

"I thought you were home."

There's no reply, just the wind scraping branches across the window.

"Dad?"

Again, no reply. A squirrel clambers up the side of the hut, onto the roof. I hear the trees shaking their limbs.

I poke my head out of the sleeping bag and look around the room. Nothing. I turn on my back and look up at the ceiling. Although my eyes have adjusted, the room is still very dark.

There is a sudden constriction around my heart. Tears pinch at the back of my eyes. I have not been able to cry since he died, not even at the funeral, where we buried a portion of him in the form of ash. I have kept a small vial of his ashes to carry with me. It is right now lying at the foot of my mat in the outer pocket of my backpack. Is that why he visited? Because I've been carrying him with me these last three months?

Within a week I am able to sit for an hour without moving, but my hips and legs ache and there is a snarl of muscle in my upper back that feels like a knife wound. I am always worried that the bandage might fall down, or that I might run out of my hut for the early morning meditation and forget to put it on. But so far that hasn't happened.

We are observing what Somchai calls "noble silence," which means we don't talk much. A couple of times I have forgotten to deepen my voice, but only when speaking a word or two—no one seemed to notice, just as no one seems to notice that I don't have an Adam's apple. In fact, other than John's probing glance on the first day, no one really looks at me. We have been instructed to interact as little as possible, to go deep into ourselves and practice as if we are in isolation.

Although we observe noble silence, overall the monastery is not as strict as the website led me to believe. The online schedule listed three meditation periods a day, each to be announced fifteen minutes beforehand by the ringing of a bell: "The morning bell rings at 4:45 a.m., and meditation begins promptly at 5:00 a.m. in the meditation hall." Yet we have not sat at five any morning since I arrived. Tep is the bell-ringer, and I usually hear him outside my hut at around six. By 6:15 we are all assembled in the hall, and Som usually arrives by 6:20. Contrary to the online schedule, there is no group meditation in the afternoon, and the 5:00 – 6:00 evening meditation usually only lasts half an hour. The final meditation is always followed by Somchai's discourse, which is supposed to last another hour, although it never lasts more than fifteen minutes. In these talks, which are more like chats, Somchai never mentions Buddha or the sutras. He might talk about some early spring flower he saw in the woods, or a recent trip to the city in which he enjoyed an excellent mug of chai. He might remind us that soaking the beans overnight with seaweed will prevent us from stinking up the meditation hall with our gas. He laughs a lot during these discourses and, during the question period that follows, usually asks us more questions than we ask him. Sometimes he doesn't speak at all, just sits quietly for a while before getting up and going back to his hut.

Each day, after the morning meditation, I take a big broom from the kitchen closet and use it to sweep the hall. The floor of the hall is never really dirty—usually just a few stray fluffs of dust or a sprinkling of pine needles that have fallen off someone's socks. I enjoy the soothing sound of the sweeping and the deeper silence underneath, the sunlight coming in through the big windows, the golden paths it makes on the hardwood floor.

At the end of the first week, I encounter a potato bug near the door of the hall. I entice it onto the dustpan and lift it carefully. As I push through the heavy wooden doors, I'm not looking where I'm going and almost knock the bug off when I bump into Somchai. It scurries back and forth across the dustpan as if trapped in a prison cell. I bend down to set it on the ground, saying, "It's okay, it's okay, you're going to be safe."

Seeing the bug's agitation, Somchai smiles. "Ah. Fear of death."

I am confused. The bug's anxious scurrying does not make me think of death, but then, I am not being carried on a small piece of plastic by some creature hundreds of times bigger than me.

"Fear of change," Somchai continues, stepping down the stairs onto the grass. "Same thing."

I carefully set the dustpan on the grass so the bug can crawl off. As I straighten up, Somchai asks, "And you? How is the meditation?"

"It's going okay," I lie. In fact, I have been feeling more frustrated each day but have been too afraid to approach him about it. Each time I sit on the mat, I am disturbed and angered by my mind, its frantic and insane thoughts and its seeming inability to stop thinking. I have not been sleeping well, due to nightmares of earthquakes, tsunamis, my father crashing cars into the ocean. This exhaustion makes it difficult to concentrate, and more than once I have nodded off while sitting.

"How are you meditating?" he asks me, looking attentively at my face.

I look down at the ground, feeling like a fraud. I wish I had some urgent business in the kitchen to attend to, but it isn't yet time to prepare the midday meal, and the sweeping of the hall is finished. There's nothing to do, nowhere to go. I look at the dustpan in my hand. "I don't really know," I finally say.

Somchai laughs heartily and pats me on the back. "Good, good. Not knowing. A good place to start. I sat for two years. Bruised." He points to his behind. "Then Ajahn Sun called me. But why wait so long?" He gestures toward the steps. "Let's go to my office."

I follow him to a small room off the meditation hall. I have never been in this room before and it is quite bare. There is a desk in the corner with a lamp on it, a small wooden stool pushed underneath. In the centre of the room are two meditation cushions facing one another. A small window over the desk emits some light, but other than that, the room is dim. Somchai settles down on one of the cushions and motions for me to do the same.

"Let's sit," he says.

I want to say that we have been sitting together all week and I still don't know how to meditate, but instead I quietly take the mat facing him and sit down, crossing my legs and placing my hands on my knees. I am too shy to look at him, so I stare at my lap.

"Close your eyes," Somchai says. I close them for a moment, and then open them to see what Somchai is doing. His eyes are closed and his face looks peaceful. I hurriedly close mine again.

After a couple of moments, Somchai speaks. "Just breathe normally."

I notice that my breath is a little faster than usual and I try to slow it down. I feel embarrassed at my own nervousness. I hope the dimness of the room makes my expression difficult to read.

"As you breathe, watch the breath. It goes in, it leaves. Feel it tickle your nose, right inside. Notice it coming and going, but do not follow it up the nose. Let's try for a while."

Again, we sit together in silence. I am aware that my breath has slowed slightly, but my heart is still beating quickly. I curse it in my mind. Then I remind myself that I should be kind. I should be thankful for my heart, for all the work it does to keep me alive. Even though I don't want to, I start thinking of my father.

"Then the thoughts," Somchai continues. "Don't get distracted. If a thought comes, let it go, but don't follow it. Just watch the breath."

It was my mother who found him. They hadn't lived together for years, but she still had the keys to his apartment. When he missed their tea date, she went to check on him and found him sitting on the couch, a calm expression on his face, his hands resting in his lap as if meditating. He hadn't grabbed his chest; he hadn't slumped forward or toppled over. He hadn't even been reading one of his spiritual books or watching TV. He was just sitting alone after work and his heart gave up. Did he know it was coming? Was that why he looked so peaceful?

I try to return to my breath. All week, my mind has felt torn in a thousand directions. Memories of my father mix with angry thoughts about ex-girlfriends, tattoos I hope to design, recipes for chilli I thought I had forgotten and now want to make for the monks. I wonder if there are enough onions and beans in the pantry, enough cayenne and paprika; I hate the feeling of the bandage squeezing my chest; I hope my mother doesn't try to contact me while I am here. Each time a new thought arrives, I jump on its back and let it take me away. All week I have been dragged through countless fantasies, have travelled down endless roads of self-aggrandizing and self-loathing, and I have grown incredibly tired of my mind's stories. I have felt helpless, I have not known what to do—but I have learned to keep my face neutral and not to shift my position.

Now I am wondering: Why has Somchai waited an entire week to instruct me? Did he make the others wait this long? Is it because he knows I am not one of them? Maybe he knows how unhappy I am. What if he can read my mind? The minute I think this, I know it's ridiculous, but I still feel a splinter of fear that it might be true.

"Nothing to be afraid of," Somchai says in a soothing tone. "It's just the mind."

I open my eyes a crack to look at him. His face looks so calm it makes me want to break something. It is easy, apparently, for Somchai to say it is just the mind. But what could be more terrifying? It might have been my mind that conjured up my father's ghost. I can't be sure.

We sit together in silence for several more minutes, until Somchai finally says, "Enough. That's enough for today. See how it goes this evening. We'll talk tomorrow."

Late that night, I dream I am running through a burnt-out village, wearing the shreds of the pink nightgown my mother bought for my thirteenth birthday. I desperately need to pee, but there are no bathrooms, and I can't crouch down somewhere because the people everywhere with peeling skin will see me. I wake with a start, my bladder full. I do not want to walk through the darkness to the one bathroom in the main building, but I am also too afraid to bare my bum to the undergrowth and the night.

As I ease open the door to the main building, I hear rustling in the kitchen. A thief? A bear? Tep told me that last summer a bear reached into the kitchen window and swiped a pie that was cooling on the counter. After a day alone with my mind, I do not want to encounter any other wild animals. I walk cautiously to the door and peer in. The overhead light burns fluorescent and there is Som, leaning over the counter, spooning chocolate ice cream from a large tub into his mouth. He is eating slowly, and there are smears of chocolate on his lips. He stares down at the tub with a slight smile on his face and doesn't see me as I creep back to the door.

The next day, Somchai doesn't call for me. I meditate alone in my hut, wearing an old tee shirt of my father's and a pair of boxers. My breasts are unbound and I feel freer than I have in days, the breath moving effortlessly through me—it seems to stream out of my fingertips and the top of my head. I don't want to be anywhere else, doing anything else.

Then an itching starts in my left ear, above my eyebrow, at the back of my neck. I will myself not to scratch it, to keep my hands in my lap.

My hair is starting to grow in a little bit. I will have to borrow a razor from one of the monks. I want to reach up and run my hand over my scalp—it is comforting to feel the soft down, like stroking some little animal.

I used to have long black hair that men always wanted to touch. In cafes, on the train or in the street, I tried to dodge their hands. If they managed to touch a strand, I would whip my hair over my shoulder and hiss. Sometimes it wasn't men. Sometimes it was old white women with tight perms or too-smiley young mothers whose children thought the shiny curtain was theirs to caress.

Later, while still in my teens, I shaved my head, and then children on buses and in city parks would tug their parents' sleeves and ask, "Girl? Boy?" At them I would smile, making them giggle and turn shyly away.

I could never be invisible. When I was a child, my mother wanted me to be her little doll; she dressed me in tiny kimonos, put pink ribbons in my hair for strangers to gawk at. My father didn't approve; he loved the tomboy in me, used to call me his *musuko-musume*, his son-daughter.

Alone now in my hut, I am relieved that no one stares at me. No one tries to grab at me or comment on my appearance. There is no mother to cry, as mine did when I shaved my head, "Why are you doing this to me?" It had taken several conversations with my father before she could begin to understand that my hair had nothing to do with her. Ever since I could remember, she had tried to hold me close, to seek out my eyes in every situation.

I wake up in the middle of the night, afraid. My hat fell off while

I was sleeping, and my ears and nose are chilled. I can't see much in the darkness, but hear the creaking of trees outside, wind moving through the branches. In the corner of the room, near the door, a presence again. I feel a shiver of fear, but vow, this time, to be braver. Taking a deep breath, I sit up and try to see, but I can't make out anything. Then the presence is next to me and it feels like there is a consoling hand resting on my shoulder.

"I'm sorry," his words pulse in my mind.

I feel my heart constrict. "It's okay."

"You feel I left too early."

"It's okay. I just miss you."

"I miss you too. Are you alright?"

I pause. "I think so."

"And your mother?"

"Mom? I don't know. Haven't you visited her?"

There is a shift in his presence, a sort of sad shrug. "She can't feel me in this form."

"Oh."

"Please tell her I love her and I'm okay."

I don't reply. I stare down at my hands, even though I can't see them. It's cold in the room and I'm tempted to burrow back into my sleeping bag.

"Whenever you see her. There's no hurry. But if you do see her, tell her."

I hesitate. "Okay," I finally say.

"I'll go now. Just think of me if you need me."

"You'll come?"

"If I can, but even if I can't, think of me and you will feel my love."

"Okay."

"I love you, Misaki, very much." His presence is already starting to fade. In a few seconds, the room is clear again.

There are goose bumps on my arms—I am quite cold. I lie back down and pull the sleeping bag over my head. But I can't fall back asleep. I have no idea what time it is, but the air has the quality of pre-dawn—more a feeling than a shade of light. Soon the sun will rise and Tep will ring the bell.

After sweeping the hall, I want to find Somchai, but feel hesitant after our last meeting. He hasn't called for me, and I don't want to disturb him. I creep toward his office and stand outside the door, listening. From inside comes the sound of crinkling— a wrapper? Then I hear shuffling and suddenly the door opens and there is Somchai. I feel like a spy caught in the act. Somchai is chewing, a partially eaten chocolate bar in his hand. He waves me in and proffers the bar. I break off a piece and put it in my mouth, letting it melt. He gestures for me to sit down, and then he sits across from me, setting the chocolate on the floor beside him next to a small gold bell.

He smiles at me, not expectantly. That is one thing I have noticed about Somchai: He never seems to expect anything.

I suck the last bit of chocolate as it dissolves. The familiar sweetness calms me and I'm able to speak. "I've been wanting to ask you something."

He nods encouragingly.

"My father..."

He nods again.

"He...do you believe in ghosts?"

Somchai looks around the room, as if there might be a legion of ghosts with us at this very moment. He looks back at me and smiles. "Believe. Yes. They come here." He waves a hand nonchalantly in the air. "Sometimes they come here."

"What...what do you do when they come?"

He laughs. "Nothing."

"You don't talk to them?"

"Talk?" Somchai looks incredulous, as if I've just asked him if he rides dragons before breakfast. "No."

"Oh."

"Why?"

"My dad's ghost visited me twice since I've been here."

Somchai beams. "Good news. He is happy, right?"

"Yes." I am surprised to hear my answer. "I mean, I think so."

"Good, good. Some family ghosts come here to feel this place. It is nice because we practice. This brings some spirits. Usually good."

"What should I do if he comes again?"

"You think he will come again?"

"I don't think so," I admit.

"Okay. Then don't worry." He offers me another piece of chocolate, and when I shake my head, breaks off another piece for himself. "Anything else?"

I look down at my hands in my lap, suddenly self-conscious again. "There's one more thing."

"Yes?"

"My dad asked me to give a message to my mother, but my mother and I don't talk."

Somchai contemplatively chews his chocolate.

"I don't want to talk to her, but I want to honour my dad's request," I continue.

He continues to chew, looking serious.

"I guess I should just do it. Next time I go to the city."

He shrugs. "If you wish. The important thing is not to visit. The important thing is to forgive."

"Forgive her for what?"

"You tell me."

"There's nothing to forgive. She was a good mother." Why am I lying to him?

He shrugs. "Then visit. Give the message."

I start to speak, but Somchai picks up the small bell and rings it. "Time's up," he says. "Usually we only meet for fifteen minutes. Come tomorrow if you have more questions."

I rise to my feet, worrying that I have annoyed him and wasted his time.

"And don't worry," he says, as he leads me to the door.

That night I dream my mother is living in the monastery and also trying to pass as a man. She has shaved her blonde hair and bound her breasts and wears a red robe like Somchai's. She has taken over my kitchen chores and the sweeping of the hall. I am so angry that I scream at her during morning meditation, and Somchai kicks me out. I hike back to the road, and then realize

I have forgotten my backpack with the vial of my father's ashes. I try to go back to retrieve it, but the trail has changed—all of the paths keep dead-ending; I keep taking wrong turns. I am lost, wandering the woods without a coat or hat, while my mother peacefully meditates at the top of the mountain.

The next day, Somchai comes to me as I am scrubbing pots in the kitchen. Suchart has already wrapped up the leftovers and gone to his hut to meditate. Tep is wiping the counters, but when he sees Somchai, he hangs up the rag and quietly slips out the back door. Somchai picks up a sponge and starts washing spoons. For several moments, he doesn't say anything. After rinsing the final spoon and setting it in the dish rack, he turns to me. I am still slowly scrubbing stuck rice from the bottom of a pot.

"So, what did you decide?" he asks.

"Decide about what?"

He raises his eyebrows.

"I can't see her," I blurt out. I had barely talked to my mother at the funeral. Her crying had annoyed me, and my father's sister had been the one to comfort her while I hid in the corner next to the food table, stuffing melon balls into my mouth. I left as soon as I could.

Somchai doesn't reply; he just looks at me kindly.

I return to scrubbing the pot, wishing he would leave.

"Can you feel gratitude?" he gently asks. "Gratitude for her, even if she hurt you?"

I shrug. My shoulders hunch forward as if to protect my heart.

I want to be left alone, to clean and think. I can't bring myself to look in Somchai's eyes, but I know without looking that they have a hint of laughter in them.

Somchai pats me on the shoulder and walks toward the door. I hear him stop to open the freezer and take something out. There is the sound of a wrapper tearing as he walks to the back-door, carefully closing the door behind him.

After several weeks, I have settled into a routine. Meditating, cooking, cleaning, walking, sleeping. The monks take tea together at seven each evening, and I usually join them. We are not supposed to eat food after the midday meal, but Somchai has decreed that candy is not food, so we usually nibble on chocolate or candied ginger as we sit around the large table in the kitchen, sipping green tea. Occasionally one of the monks might tell a story or crack a joke, but usually we sit in comfortable silence.

One evening I gather my courage to retell a Buddhist story I read earlier in the day about a monk who carries a woman across a river and his fellow monk who is shocked by this. "I put down that woman a long time ago," the monk tells his prudish companion. "Why are you still carrying her?" I am thinking of how to introduce the story when Rolf yawns, carefully covering his mouth with the back of his hand. This sets off a round of yawns. Each man yawns differently, I notice. John opens his mouth wide like a tiger baring its teeth. Tep's mouth contorts to one side and Suchart looks like he is gulping air. Watching, I feel a great affection for each of them and decide there is no need to interrupt this sweet silence by telling a story. I feel a yawn coming on and open my mouth to join them.

One early May morning, I slip out after breakfast with a bucket of water and a piece of rag. There is only one bathroom in the monastery, and the shower is broken, which means my only option is a bath—but the tub is grimy and stained. So every few days, I sneak deep into the woods where a grove of vine maples curves overhead and grows back into the ground, where no one will see me.

In the grove, I take off my pants and boxers and scrub myself, then put back on my boxers and pull off my shirt, unrolling the bandage to work on my upper half. It's a cold spring; I am shivering, and try to wash quickly. Rubbing my armpits with the rag, I hear a rustle that doesn't sound like wind in the leaves. I freeze, afraid to turn my head. Birdsong. But no breeze. Then a branch cracks as if under someone's foot. I turn to see Somchai standing a short distance from me. He is looking in the other direction, leaning on his walking stick.

I instinctively cross my arms over my chest, but then just as quickly let them fall to my side. He must have already seen me. There is no use hiding now.

Somchai turns toward me. He looks briefly at my chest and then averts his eyes.

"So you're a woman," he says.

I shrug.

"A man with breasts?"

I can't help it—I laugh. "Sort of."

He looks at me questioningly.

I hesitate, and then continue. "I mean, I'm mostly a woman, but sometimes I feel like more of a man. I'm both, I guess, but more on the side of woman."

He takes a couple of steps closer and stares at my face. His look is curious and kind. "It's no problem." He pauses. The slight wrinkles around his brown eyes relax as if gently sighing. "Same name?"

"Oh. Sure. Mikio still, I guess. I mean..." I hadn't thought of this, using my real name. But why not? "Actually, Misaki, if you don't mind. My father chose it."

"Misaki." He says it slowly, and then smiles. "Nice."

I turn to quickly pull my shirt over my head before turning back with a shy smile. "Now you know," I say.

"Yes." He makes a strange little flourish with his hand, a sort of dainty twirl that I take to mean "such is the mystery of life" or something like that. He looks at me again, more penetratingly. "But why pretend?"

"I thought you only take men here."

He laughs. "Who said this?"

"Your website."

He laughs again. "Website."

"Didn't you know?"

He shrugs. "A long time ago the website was made."

"But... Buddhism... I mean, I thought Buddhism... most kinds of Buddhism don't allow monks and nuns to live together."

He smiles and pokes the ground with his walking stick. Then

he looks around and takes a deep breath, as if he is seeing and breathing the forest for the first time. "Buddhist." He holds the word like a little bit of fluff on the tip of his finger. "No, I am not that." He smiles. "You should stay. Or, if you leave, come back. You are welcome here." He looks at my tee shirt and boxers, then gestures at his worn robe, seamed from myriad darnings. "I should get some clothes. Some pants, a shirt...soon." He shrugs again and smiles, then, leaning on his stick, slowly walks away.

The grove seems colder after he leaves. The maples arc over me like the ceiling of a leafy cathedral. I breathe deeply, smelling the ground and the leaves, the whole forest. It seems like the trees and I are breathing together, and I feel a lightness in my chest. The bandage lies unwrapped, curling across the forest floor. In the dim light it could be a snake, or a long piece of skin I've unwrapped from myself.

SEIZE

In the communal house where her brother lives, there is a basket of reading material in the bathroom on a small shelf next to the toilet—bedraggled sci-fi novels, newspapers with articles written by people who are homeless or under-housed, queer zines, New Age-y mags crammed with optimistic stories about polyamorous relationships and organic urban gardens. Before leaving Portland for Seattle this morning, Robin shoved a recent issue of *Spirit Now* in her backpack. As the bus rumbles past low industrial buildings, over a steel bridge and surging grey-green river, she studies the pages in the back that offer quotes related to this issue's theme, "transformation." "Horace was the first person to write *carpe diem*, which means 'seize the day,'" she reads. "When we seize the day, we transform it. We make anew." She wonders if the rest of the issue is going to be this insultingly obvious. She turns the page.

Her reading is interrupted by a strangled sound from across

the aisle. She looks over to see a very tall, very pale young man rear up like a horse, then twist his head from side to side, moaning. He's having a manic break, is her first thought, followed by: I hope he doesn't kill us. He falls back into his seat and starts shaking violently.

In the front of the bus, a woman rises up from her seat and looks back, then strides toward the man. She is African American, dressed in black; a nose ring glints in one nostril. In front of Robin, an older woman who looks like a tourist, skin tinged fake-tan orange, leans over her husband. "Is he having a seizure?" she asks the woman in black.

"Yes," the woman answers calmly. The shaking man has slumped to the side, and his head thumps against the window. The sound resonates throughout the bus. The woman takes off her sweatshirt and carefully props it under his head, cupping her hand under his chin so it won't dip down.

"Does anyone have a pen or something to put in his mouth?" the tourist woman calls down the aisle.

"Don't put anything in his mouth," the woman holding him says. "He could choke on it."

"But he'll choke on his tongue if we don't," the tourist woman says. "We should put him on his side and clear out his mouth. Use your finger."

"I'm not putting anything in his mouth. He might bite it off."

"But what if he chokes?"

"He's not choking. He's fine right here. He's okay." The man is still jerking violently but his groaning has ceased. Her grip on his head is careful, almost tender.

"You still dig merlot, right?" her brother Nathan asked. He hadn't even looked at the menu before ordering a bottle of it and a lager on the side. They were in a trendy Indian place in a quickly gentrifying neighbourhood in North Portland, on a street that had once been a thriving African-American community of barber and auto body shops, barbecue joints and sturdy wooden houses, before the city decided to rezone it and turn it into a late-night entertainment district. Elaborate tapestries hung on the walls and sleek glass tables gleamed in the muted light. "I had an interesting talk with Mom today. About our family history. Turns out Uncle Randy—you remember him? Turns out he had a weak liver. And he got the gout by thirty or something. Didn't even drink. Dry like Mom. But he still got sick."

The server returned with Nathan's beer and uncorked the wine, pouring them each a glass. Nathan grabbed his beer and took a long drink. "So it's nothing to worry about. It runs in the family, this liver thing."

Nathan had walked in the door that evening late from his job at the framing shop and headed straight for the fridge. He had pulled out two beers, twisted off the lids, and set one in front of her on the kitchen table as he lifted the other to his lips, taking a big chug.

"Hard day?" she had joked. This was his ritual every day, hard or not.

He shrugged. "I went to see Mom after work. She called me, wouldn't tell me what it was about. When I got there, she wanted me to mow her lawn. I told her I didn't have time. I'll do it Saturday."

"She could have asked me to do it when I was over yesterday."

"Yeah, well, welcome to the oldest son's world."

"The *only* son."

"The only son's world." They both laughed. Their mother was always trying to get men—including her son—to do things for her.

In the restaurant, Robin watched him drink his beer and was at a loss. She took a small sip of her merlot, trying to think of something neutral to say. "That's good," she finally managed. "I mean, that you found that out."

He looked at her for a long moment, as if trying to assess whether or not she was being sarcastic. Before he could reply, the waiter walked up with two steaming plates of food, setting a lentil curry in front of Nathan and saag paneer in front of Robin. They dug in, eating silently for a few moments.

"So how's work?" Robin asked.

"Oh." Nathan flicked his hand as if brushing away a fly. "You know. The usual. Lately Tamara is getting on my nerves, though. Get this: the other day, I ask a Black customer paying credit for his ID. No biggie, right? But Tamara brings it up with management. Says I never do this to white customers. What?" He took a long sip of his beer and stared down at his plate. "I mean, this is standard procedure. We tried to talk about it—she just wouldn't hear me. I just don't understand it. She's making a big deal out of nothing. It doesn't make any sense to me, so I decided just not to say anything to her." He shoved a forkful of curry in his mouth and chewed.

Robin stared at him for a minute before speaking. Finally, she said in what she hoped was a gentle tone, "Maybe you were being kind of...? You know, unconsciously?"

Nathan looked annoyed. "Kind of what? Don't be ridiculous."

"But...don't you? I mean, we're white, and we have a certain, you know...privilege, I mean..."

He looked uncomfortable. "Privilege. That's something you believe. Okay."

She couldn't believe this was her brother she was talking to. But then, he had said a number of things on this visit that had dismayed her.

He continued to chomp away at his curry. He took a chug of beer and washed it down with wine. His expression was somber, as if he was still considering her question. Finally he said, "Maybe we shouldn't talk about this. It seems like a hot topic. I don't want to make you upset. You don't come to town very often and this is supposed to be a celebration dinner." He attempted a carefree smile and raised his wineglass. "Let's cheers. To good times."

She wanted to say more, but something stopped her. She was afraid that further conversation would just make the widening gap between them even more apparent. She hesitated, and then raised her glass slowly. Their glasses chimed a sweet tone, but she avoided his eyes as they drank.

Nathan filled the silence. "Remember Tracy? She's out in Boston now. Med school. Can you believe it?" He rambled on about old friends until the server stopped by their table. By that time he had finished his beer and two glasses of wine. When the server asked if they needed anything else, Nathan ordered another beer. "And another bottle?" he asked Robin.

She laughed. "Are you kidding? I'm still finishing my glass."

He gave a small shrug without smiling. "Okay. Just the beer then," he told the server.

As Robin was sipping an after-dinner chai, Nathan swallowed the last of his third beer and excused himself. "Little boy's room. I'll be right back."

But he wasn't right back. After fifteen minutes, she asked the server if he'd mind checking the bathroom. She was worried Nathan had fallen. But the server came back with an apologetic, puzzled look on his face. "He's not there."

She paid the bill and walked out into the night. The strip was getting buzzy: groups of friends out bar-hopping, couples nuzzling their way down the street, laughter spilling from patios, a juggler setting up her pins on the corner. Robin knew where she'd find her brother. Four doors down was a seedy bar, the type frequented by hipsters with ironic moustaches. The sign outside pulsed "Old West Saloon" and had an image of a cowboy on a horse, the neon light in his lasso burnt out.

Robin pushed through the doors, hoping Nathan wasn't already on the floor. The place was packed, but she saw him immediately. He was sitting at the bar, his back to her. She knew he was doing shots, probably of Jim Beam. She stopped for a moment, listening to the beeping of the pinball machines, the swirl of conversations, the *thwack* of a pool cue hitting the ball. What would she say to him? What could she say?

She walked up and put her arm around his shoulder. "Hey bro," she said.

He turned, unsurprised, breathing cheap whisky into her face. He attempted a mischievous grin. "Busted," he said.

Two hours later, she couldn't get a taxi to stop for them. Nathan was slumped heavily on her shoulder, one arm around her neck. Finally one pulled over.

"He's not gonna puke, is he?" the driver asked. "I don't want anyone puking in my cab."

"No. He won't. I promise. Don't worry." She had no idea where her assuredness came from.

Robin glances down at the magazine open on her lap. There's a quote from a writer from the last century about butterflies, how their wings unfurl like secrets told for the first time. Jesus. She certainly picked the wrong issue to steal.

"He's bleeding! There's blood on his chin!" The tourist woman has climbed over her husband and is standing in the aisle, leaning over the woman holding his head.

"He probably just bit his tongue." The woman in black takes a tissue out of her pocket and dabs his chin. "It's not much blood. He's okay."

"Maybe we should tell the driver to pull over."

"There's no need for that. People have seizures all the time."

"But he's bleeding!"

"Not really." The woman still sounds calm. "See, he's starting to slow down." The man quivers as his head slumps forward. He starts snoring deeply, sucking air into his huge nostrils. She eases him back into his seat and repositions the sweatshirt, plumping it up like a pillow before setting his head on it.

"I still think we should pull over and call 911," the older woman says disapprovingly.

"Why? He's not seizing anymore."

"He needs medical attention." There's an edge to her voice.

"I think he's okay."

"How do you know?"

"I'm a nurse."

"Oh." The tourist woman looks deflated. She sits back down.

When they finally got home it was late, after one. Nathan barely made it through the front door before he fell to his knees and started retching. Robin ran to the kitchen to get the wastebasket and held his head over it while he threw up, thinking how glad she was his roommates weren't awake to witness this, although they'd no doubt seen it before. The smell was nauseating, and she had to breathe through her mouth to keep from throwing up with him. She tried to focus on keeping a firm grip on his head, which was difficult, as his hair was damp and his cheeks were cold from sweat. Finally he stopped heaving and slumped to the floor, his arm encircling the wastebasket.

"I'm so tired of being sick," he said. "I'm so tired." Tears ran down his face.

Robin sat beside him and patted his back. "It's okay," she said. "You're home. It's okay."

She got him to crawl over to the couch. Once on it, he promptly passed out. Robin bagged up the puke and took it out to the garbage can out back. Then she got a clean towel from a kitchen drawer and dampened it under the sink, carefully wiping off his face and neck and dabbing at the bits on his shirt.

She stared at his sleeping face. He was three years older than her, but he had always looked younger, with his fresh, unlined skin, his blue eyes curious as a little boy's. For many years he had been a vegetarian, and she had always attributed his good complexion to his diet. But now he didn't look so great. His eyes were sunken; dark half-moons drooped below them. There were wrinkles on his forehead and lines like parentheses on either side of his mouth. His skin was red and patchy, a small outcropping of zits on his chin.

A couple of days earlier, he had told her that his roommates had recently given him an ultimatum. Chill with his drinking, or move out. He had been offended. "They all drink," he told her. "I don't know why I'm being singled out." Still, he told her he planned to drink less. "I've been partying a little hard lately." He had cracked his charming grin. "You know me. Old habits die hard, etcetera, etcetera."

She had been responsive, encouraging, as she always was in their conversations. She told him about a close friend of hers who had recently joined AA. She started to share that she also felt she had to be careful with her drinking, how back home she only had one or two drinks a night, and only on weekends now, but something stopped her—a feeling, a shift in the room. She glanced at his face. He was looking away, studying a faded concert poster tacked to the living room wall. She knew the look. He was somewhere else. He had decided to tune her out.

Nathan had been the first person to arrive at her going-away party four years earlier. "Sis." He had fallen heavily into her arms and breathed whisky into her ear. He smelled of sweat and his face was grimy. He straightened himself and lurched toward her couch. "I need a drink, man! Sister's going to grad school. Gotta celebrate!"

Why hadn't she said something? She hadn't. She had just done what she usually did: she went into the kitchen and put on water for coffee.

"You got beer?" he called from the living room.

Before she could answer, the bell rang. Harjit, the first of their friends, with a bottle of gin and a bag of chips. Before Robin could brew the coffee, more friends showed up, crowding the kitchen with cocktail glasses and beer bottles. And that's how the night had gone. Nathan was slurring his words before they left the house. At the club, he yelled at the bartender and got into a fistfight with one of their friends. She had managed to drag him back to her place where he had sat in the middle of her living room floor to take off his boots and then stood up to piss in them. "Cool, huh," he had blurrily pronounced. She knew he wouldn't remember any of it in the morning and she was right.

She remembered him dancing around in tight jeans and gaudy high-tops on her twenty-fifth birthday. He had been drunk, sure, but fun. The laughter of every party—cracking jokes while passing a joint in front of the club, out on the back porch on summer evenings surrounded by friends, flipping veggie burgers with a beer in his hand. It had all seemed so effortless for him.

But then he started saying mean things, things he didn't remember saying. He borrowed money and didn't pay it back. He bit a friend's cheek so hard it left a bruise. He forgot important events, like weddings. He lost his keys about once a month, and sometimes spent the night on the front steps of his house because he couldn't figure out how to get inside. Old friends stopped calling him. He complained they'd all gotten too serious, too boring. He started spending more time alone, stopping by the store for a couple of six packs on his way home, eating nachos for dinner, watching TV until late into the night. And what had she done? She—she had moved away.

Robin looks out the window. They've left the industrial zone and are entering a stretch of farmland. Long rows of grape vines extend out in front of country houses whose white paint has worn thin. Rows of blueberry bushes undulate. She sees a sign for "U-pick" strawberries. The bus rolls on.

Across the aisle, the tall man's loud snoring has stopped. He is still slumped on the woman's sweatshirt, but his face looks peaceful. The woman has gone back to her seat and now returns with a book. She sits down beside him, opens it, and starts to read.

THE ADVENTURE

Your apartment has never been more clean. You clean a lot now. Even more than before. The cat gave you fleas so now you vacuum every week, wash all your bedding and most of your clothes. You don't leave your backpack on the floor, you dust your shoes with boric acid.

The cleaning is a comfort. There is the scrubbing of the bathtub and the stove, the sweeping (which sounds like "weeping") of the floor (the weeping of the floor), the shaking of the doormat (the shaking).

There is always so much to clean. Clean out the email folder with her name. Clean out the pictures. The sweet messages, some with emoticons and exclamation points—although she claimed to hate both. Clean her hairs out of the hairbrush, throw away the yellow sparkly toothbrush you bought for her to keep at your place. It's three weeks after and you're still finding strands of her long dark hair in your bathroom. You're not sure how this is possible.

You've cleaned the bathroom so many times. But the hairs keep showing up.

The only thing you don't clean is your body. Not regularly, at least. You used to be well-groomed, but you take pleasure now in the greasy hair, the dry skin on your legs. A few pimples have popped up near your nose. You're no teenager. But love turns us all into teenagers and so does heartbreak. And so: the pimples and the crying and the calling and hanging up when you hear her message start.

It started with a bike trip. Or rather, that's how it started to end. You'd been dating for one year and two months and were still in love. This was the longest for either of you. Assured the feeling would continue, you started planning a bike tour across Asia and Europe. It would take eight months. You would camp, hostel, sojourn. You would drink lager in Berlin and skinny dip in Thailand and sleep at the foot of snowy mountains, wrapped in each other's arms. You would hold hands and make out in cities where that was okay and exchange surreptitious, desirous glances in provincial towns where it wasn't. You would adventure and you would fall more deeply in love.

It's always the plans that undo us. We see our futures together stretching out like a long, gloriously golden road, with maybe a few potholes or muddy hills to make it interesting. There are different signposts on this road, like "moving in together," "having a child," or "taking our first vacation." Some signposts are shadowy—we can't read them, they're too far in the distance, or we don't want to read them so we pretend they're not there. Signposts like "lying about an affair" or "grieving a death" or "forgetting that which brings joy."

At first, planning the bike trip brought them both great happiness. Cuddled on her couch, the cat at their feet, they would pore over maps, tracing the routes with careful fingers. The guidebooks gave descriptions of colourful towns, bazaars and beaches, rose gardens and full-bodied wines, spicy meals served out of tiny tin shacks, views other people's cameras could never capture. They wanted to devour these experiences whole, together. To suck up life and lick their fingers. They saw each other splayed on hotel beds or sweating in fragrant vineyards. They would have these experiences and they would have each other.

This is the risk of consumption: it may consume the consumer. This happened to one of them. She got too quickly full. Of the plans. Of her lover. After dinner she did not want to talk or curl up on the couch and open the guidebooks. She wanted to read alone or watch a movie. She didn't touch the other as often. She combed her long brown hair with her fingers and thought of friends she missed and places she might like to travel alone. She stopped using the future tense and avoided the word "we."

After a few weeks of this, she asked for a talk. She asked kindly, and she said the words in the order they are always said, with the correct disclaimers. She sipped peppermint tea, she looked pained, she took all responsibility. She apologized. She apologized again. She apologetically sipped her tea and kept apologizing.

The lover who liked things clean—who had always liked things clean—watched the words slip and stutter out of the other's mouth and thought about how to clean up the mess. She thought about which natural products to use and how to get her teeth whiter and whether her mother used white vinegar or lemon juice for the kitchen counters. She thought about bloodstains on sheets and flea bites on legs and the acne scars on her newly-ex lover's neck. She thought about the toxins in her ex-lover's blood, and the toxins in her own blood, and wondered what sort of cancer each of them would die from, or if they would die from something else, and who would be with them when they died. She tried to look in her eyes and listen, to calmly hear the careful, the expected words. She tried to focus, or to at least think of something else, but she could only see the one long road splitting into two, each a little less glorious, a little less golden, each flowing separately into the sun.

THE GARDEN OF VOWS

"My doctor gave me the liquid stuff. It's good for me." He shoved a large piece of fudge into his mouth and chewed loudly while his other hand loosely held the steering wheel. We had already stopped at two drive-throughs before the chocolate outlet store. The car was littered with hamburger wrappers and empty cigarette packs.

"It would have been hard for me to quit on my own," he continued. "But then, I crashed the car at work and had to get my blood tested. So it's good for me, I guess. I mean, if that hadn't happened, I wouldn't be doing this. I'd just be at home, like, getting high and probably eating candy." He laughed. "Like I am now." He grabbed another piece of fudge from the box balanced between us and crammed it into his mouth. "Except I'm not high." He laughed again. "Not for two weeks."

I looked out the window. The interstate was packed; cars streamed by on either side of us, the hot sun glinting off the hoods.

We were passing yet another string of depressingly uniform strip malls. We had been driving for two hours.

He rambled on. "That's what I love about Zen. The silence, you know. I missed it the last few years. The sitting. Zazen. And the walking, of course. I love it all. Even the oryoki. Although I can never fold my napkin right. And the light in the zendo is fantastic. Wait 'til you see it. I love to meditate in there. It's like Dōgen Zenji said: We all have to sit down. Not just monks. You know Dōgen Zenji, right?"

"Is he the head monk or something?"

He laughed and shook his head, grabbing another piece of fudge. He answered while chewing, his mouth full of white goo. "He was the founder of Zen. Or one school of it or something. I think. I can't remember all the details, but my teacher in Eugene used to talk about him, how he was the one who got everyone sitting on their zafus."

"Zafus?"

"Cushions. For meditating. I have one at home. Although I don't really practice at home. Not much, anyway. Not lately."

A huge soda and an extra large coffee were crammed in the beverage holders. The coffee had been cooling for the last half hour, but he didn't seem to mind. He grabbed the soda and sucked on the straw. "I still dream of being a monk. Getting away from it all. Living in peace."

"Don't they work too, these monks and nuns?" I asked.

"Oh sure," he said. "They work some. Gardening and such. Cooking maybe. I'd work too. If someone asked me to. But really I think I'd work best by sitting. It's my dream to be the doan.

That's the one who rings the bell." He nudged the box of fudge in my direction. "Want some?"

"No thanks." I looked back out the window. Only three more hours until we reached our destination. If we got there. He had already almost hit two cars, at one point veering into the other lane to avoid rear-ending the car in front of us. While eating his double hamburgers, he had steered with his knees. He was surprised when I asked him to stop. He did it all the time, he said. It was perfectly safe. But when I threatened to get out and hitch, he agreed to keep at least one hand on the wheel.

We had only met that morning. I had contacted him through the monastery's ride board earlier in the week. I had wanted to do a retreat for a long time and this week was perfect. I was desperate to get away from the apartment—I didn't want to come home from work to Sofia's unbearably distant kindness, didn't want to sit on the couch and watch her pack boxes.

"I'm Brad," he had said, as soon as I sat down in the passenger seat. "And you don't have to worry. I'm a good driver."

We passed a sign for the military museum. We were nearing the state's largest army base. An antique canon was positioned carefully in the middle of a large field, and I could see a few old tanks some distance behind it.

Brad glanced over at the canon. "My father was there."

"At the museum?"

"No, at the base. Before Vietnam. He only has four fingers. I mean four fingers on one of his hands."

Even though I didn't feel like talking, I found myself saying, "That must have been hard."

"What?"

"Having a dad who was a Vietnam vet."

"Oh, it wasn't too bad. I mean, he wasn't violent or nothing." He lit an extra wide cigarette and took a deep drag, exhaling a bellow of smoke.

"Do you mind opening the window?" I asked.

"Oh yeah, sure, sorry." He hurriedly unrolled the window and the traffic sounds poured in. He took another drag. "He was pretty depressed though."

We sat in silence after that. After a few minutes, Brad fiddled with the radio, finding a station that played classic rock.

"This okay?"

"Sure."

"Silence is good, but in small doses." He laughed.

I didn't say anything. We had only been silent for four or five minutes, and we were about to enter a full week of silence. But he had been to the monastery before. He knew what he was getting into I assumed.

He turned down the music. "The thing about my dad, though," he continued, "is that he got happier after my mom left. Not a lot, but a little. You'd think it would be the opposite. But it wasn't. It must have still been hard on him, though. I mean, she left him for another woman. That must have been hard on him, as a man, you know. I never thought about that before."

Hard on him as a man. I had things to say about that. Why would being left for a woman be worse than being left for a man?

Maybe his father took it as an affront to his masculinity—he hadn't been "man" enough, so his wife turned lesbian. Who knew? I didn't have the energy to engage Brad on the subject. I had barely slept the entire last week.

I looked back out the window. More strip malls. Outlet stores and car dealerships and gas stations. Small rectangles of flattened grass surrounded by parking lots. A few sickly-looking trees, the blue sky far overhead.

Brad continued. "I was only eleven. When she left, I didn't know what was up. The house was just empty and she only came every other weekend. My dad was usually at work. That's when I started getting high. Just pot, you know, with buddies after school. No one was ever around to stop me."

I had avoided looking at him for most of the drive, but now I turned to look at his face. He had pouchy cheeks and a wide forehead. His gaze was focused on the road, so I couldn't see into his eyes, but there were bags under them. Bits of food were caught at the corners of his mouth. His hair was still mussed from sleep. He dressed like a teenager, oversized jeans and a baggy tee shirt, but his face was already aging. I guessed he was in his mid-twenties.

I didn't know what to say. I didn't want to pry by asking more questions, and I had no desire to console him, to make him feel better about his childhood or his addiction. I had had enough of playing counsellor in my own life. From what I could tell, Brad was just a confused kid. There was a lot he hadn't yet thought about. His parents' pain was still a mystery to him, as was his own. He had a long road ahead of him.

We drove on in uncomfortable silence, punctuated by the sound of Brad slurping away at his soda. I looked at my watch. It was only eleven in the morning. Right now Sofia would be getting up and making coffee, reading through the paper. She would have already fed the cats. She might be checking email, or making a call to her lover. "Yes, she's away for a week," I could hear her voice saying. "I'm sure I'll find a place before she gets back."

The monastery was in an old elementary school, with long shadowy halls and big draughty rooms. Brad and I reported to the cafeteria where several other meditators were waiting. We were signed in by a youngish man with a long, red beard who introduced himself as Peter and gave us copies of the week's schedule. I glanced over it. Morning bell at 5:00 a.m., lunch at 11:00 a.m., interviews with the teachers at 3:00 p.m, dinner at 5:00 p.m., lights out at 10:00 p.m. And in between: hours upon hours of meditation.

Brad disappeared to his room. Peter introduced me to a gentle shaved-headed woman in an orange and red robe named Jaspreet. She led me down the labyrinth of halls to the women's dormitory and told to me to report to the zendo at 5:00 p.m. "Noble silence begins then," she whispered.

It was my luck to be seated only two cushions down from Brad. It was there that I encountered his feet. A rotting graveyard, the deadest of animals, the dankest pit of a groin—his feet did not simply smell unwashed; it was as if they were completely overtaken by some fungus growing out from the very centre of the bone. I didn't know how I had managed to avoid this smell on the ride down. It must have been sealed up in his sneakers, any stray wafts concealed by the smell of cigarettes, burgers, and coffee.

The teachers were older, with shaved heads and kind faces. Roshi Tamiko and Roshi Leonard. They gave us meditation instructions. We were to keep our eyes slightly open, and slightly unfocused, directing our gaze to the floor about two feet in front of us. If we had to close our eyes, we could. We were not to repeat any mantras or prayers. We were simply to follow the breath in and out.

"Your awareness is like a sentinel guarding the gate of your nostrils. You are aware of the guest—the breath—as it enters the gate and as it leaves, but you don't follow the guest inside the gate. Your job is to simply be aware of it entering and leaving," Roshi Tamiko said in a calm, measured voice.

The light spilled from floor-to-ceiling windows over the hardwood floor. The large room was silent, save for a few rustles as the meditators settled on their cushions. I tried to focus on my breath, but each time I breathed in, I could only smell Brad's feet. The smell was nauseating. I couldn't focus. My mind wandered to thoughts of Sofia, her slender fingers, nails painted grey or coral or sea green. She was typing on her computer, looking for apartments online. She was reading a text from her lover and laughing. She was imagining what plants she would buy to decorate her new place.

In the afternoons, we were given an hour to nap or wander the grounds. On the first two days, I slept, but on the third I felt more energetic and decided to take a walk. In back of the monastery was a large garden that provided much of the produce for our meals. I wandered the rows, looking at the spinach and collards, the zucchinis and tomatoes. I pinched off a leaf of oregano and held it to my nose. Beyond the garden was a large hill with a giant Buddha statue on top of it. I decided to climb up for a better look.

The Buddha was made of wood and had recently been repainted gold. There were a few offerings at the statue's feet. A candle, a little scroll of paper tied with green ribbon, a dried rose. The statue's hands were huge, facing up towards the sky, the index fingers touching the thumbs. I had learned from Roshi Tamiko the day before that this was called a *mudra*. I looked down the other side of the hill and saw a tangle of trees and bushes with objects dangling from the branches. Two trees with a cloth banner slung between them formed an entryway arch.

As I got closer, I saw that there were words sewn into the banner with red thread: "The Garden of Great Vows."

Inside this garden were lavender and sage bushes, small aspens and apple trees. The ground was thick with weeds and moss. Wildflowers sprung up between rocks. The narrow pathways were overgrown. It was the most crowded garden I had ever been in—but not because of the plants. The trees and bushes were full of hanging bits of cloth and paper and the ground was littered with painted stones, pieces of tile and wood. On each stone, each piece of cloth, were words. "I vow to be a good parent." "I vow to eat meat only once a week." "I will cherish the earth." "I vow to follow the eightfold path." "I vow to keep my heart open."

Some vows I could only read parts of because the paper had disintegrated or the paint had worn off. These partial vows were the most interesting to me. They were like fragments of poems. "Vow...sober." "ow to be kin." "I...present." "Love...for...er."

I heard the bell calling us back to meditate, but I didn't return to the hall. I stayed in the garden for a long time, touching the stones and pieces of wood, unrolling the curled slips of paper, tracing the words with my fingers. I read every vow and then started to reread them. I stayed all afternoon, until the sun started to go down and the shadows lengthened and the lavender and rosemary gave off a sweet rich smell. The branches of the trees rustled, touching each other. And then I heard the dinner bell.

On the fourth day, the teachers gave us more detailed instructions on meditation.

"You must watch your minds," Roshi Leonard reminded us. "Don't let your mind trick you into straying from your breath. Your breath is your friend, your companion, and you must stay with it at all times.

"You have already learned how tricky your minds are," Roshi Leonard continued. "Crazy little monkeys—our minds. Monkey mind. Rushing this way and that, grabbing one object and then throwing it down and grabbing another. Again and again. Monkey mind."

I imagined a monkey climbing a tree, grabbing coconuts and

throwing them at my head. I ducked and wrapped my arms around my head, but the monkey kept hurling coconuts. I ran away from the tree and bumped into Sofia. She was carrying a very heavy suitcase and it dragged on the ground. I tried to help her lift it up, but just then, a coconut crashed against my ear.

"Monkey mind is not to be underestimated. It is the biggest obstacle on the path. Your mind." There was the slightest sheen of sweat on his brown face, but he spoke calmly as he adjusted the neck of his red robe. "Today we are asking that you pay more attention to your feet. During walking meditation, concentrate on your feet as well as your breath. Pay attention to each toe as it touches the ground, pay attention to your heels as they touch the cool wood. Notice where the wood is a bit warmer from the sunshine—notice that sensation. Remember to walk carefully. Each heel should land just in front of your toes."

The person sitting next to me had disappeared on the third day. Since we couldn't talk, I had no way of asking what had happened to her. She had probably gotten sick of the silence. Or else she'd felt oppressed by the repetitious rigidity of the practice, the bowing to Buddha statues, the bowing to teachers, the bowing to fellow meditators, the bowing to one's own meditation cushion. Perhaps she had gotten bored of the slow ceremonial meals, where each item was eaten in a certain order, at a certain time— even the way one folded their napkin was dictated by custom. I myself was so tired of these meals that I could barely stand to rinse the leftover rice from my bowl with tea and drink it as we were instructed to. I had to continually remind myself that it was better than being at home.

Since my neighbour was gone, I had to follow directly behind Brad during walking meditation. Although I knew I was supposed to concentrate on my own feet, I kept staring at his. They were like no feet I had ever seen before. Completely covered with a red rash, they also sported patches of white peeling skin. They looked like the feet of a plague victim, or some spiritually unenlightened person who had been scorched trying to walk over hot coals. Their stink had not abated since the first day; in fact, it seemed worse. I had resigned myself to breathing only through my mouth.

We walked slowly around the hall in a figure-eight pattern. I held my hands at belly-button level, one loosely cupped in the other, thumbs touching, just as I had been taught. I tried to feel the boards under my feet and to watch my breath like a sentinel at the gate. But there was Sofia again, in a bright pink dress and black heels, standing by a wrought iron gate and merrily waving. She had a different suitcase this time, a small green one that she swung from one hand as if it weighed nothing. In her other hand was a piece of paper. A letter? To me?

"Keep your mind on your breath. Follow your feet," Roshi Leonard intoned.

I tried to return my attention to my breath. My feet moved underneath me as if they belonged to someone else. I couldn't feel my soles on the floor. I couldn't feel anything. I walked and tried to pay attention. Suddenly there was a tightening in my chest, water stinging my eyes.

I knew what the letter meant. But I had known that before I ever got in the car to come to this place.

On the sixth day, Roshi Tamiko prepared us to break the silence. Sitting on her red cushion, she lifted a small copper bowl and hit it with a small wooden mallet, letting the chime resonate throughout the room. When it had completely died down, she spoke. "Tomorrow you will speak to each other," she said, looking around the sunlit room at our tired and expectant faces. "And I want to encourage you to move very slowly, in your actions and in your conversations. Don't rush into anything. Don't speak too quickly. Hold each other very gently in your speaking and think kindly before you speak.

"We are going to practice a new kind of meditation to prepare for this breaking of silence." She shifted on her cushion. "It is called The Mother Meditation. Some of you who come here often have practiced it before. But for the newcomers, I will explain it again. It goes like this. In your mind, you call up a picture of your mother's face. The kindest version of your mother possible. If you had a terribly unkind mother, then use another kind face— perhaps the face of a beloved aunt or grandmother. Some kind face. Hold this face in your mind and feel your love for this person. Let it grow inside you. Feel it in your heart.

"Now, imagine yourself in a place from your daily life back home. It could be the office you work in or a classroom in a school you attend. It could be the bus you take to work each day. Imagine yourself there. Look around. Carefully, slowly, look around at each person. Look at each person's face. And as you look at them, imagine that they are your mother. Feel that love in your heart. Imagine each person has your mother's kind face. Feel gratitude for this person who gave birth to you, who brought you into the world through her body. Feel thankful for the life you have. For each person in front of you." Roshi Tamiko looked around the room again. "Now, let's practice." She straightened her back, half-closed her eyes, and settled into silence.

I kept my eyes open. I wasn't yet ready to meditate. I wanted to think.

I knew I was one of the lucky ones. I actually had a kind mother, one who sent me sweaters she hadn't knitted herself, nice-looking sweaters I actually liked, that actually fit me, and books, good books she had actually read. She knew when to ask me questions and when to offer advice and when to just let me cry.

But what about all the people in this room who didn't have a mother like that, and who didn't have a kind aunt or a kind grandmother? I surreptitiously glanced around the room at the other meditators. People of various ethnicities; young, old, middle-aged; women, ambiguously gendered, men—all sat in silence, their eyes closed or nearly closed, glancing downward. I was the only one looking around.

I had forgotten to breathe through my mouth and I suddenly smelled Brad's feet again, putrefying and sharp. Disgust and annoyance surged through me. Then I remembered something.

I had entered the zendo behind him that morning, just in time to see him slip off his shoes—a pair of scuffed, blackened sneakers that had once been white, pushed down at the heels so that they resembled slippers. He had paused at the door and lifted the shoes up onto a shelf, placing them carefully next to someone's elaborately embroidered green slippers. The carefulness of this gesture surprised me. In the first days we had been at the monastery, I had more than once seen Brad hastily kick off his stinking shoes and scurry into the zendo right before the final bell was rung. But this morning he had taken his time, placing the shoes with care.

Was Brad my mother, someone to be grateful to? I paused on this thought, remembering to breathe through my mouth. He hadn't had much of a mother himself, from the sound of it.

And what about Sofia?

After we moved in together, her mother used to call our apartment and leave sobbing messages: "Puta! Disgusting whore. Never call again."

I had tried to downplay it, had even, foolishly, made a joke about it. Sofia had been furious. I tried to convince Sofia that her mom didn't really mean it, that she would eventually get over it and welcome Sofia back, welcome us into her life. But that never happened. And Sofia never forgave me for my reaction.

I felt my jaw clench, and then willed myself to relax. Slowly, I returned to my breath, imagining my mother's calm, lined face. She was grinning at me, walking towards me with a cup of strong coffee, stirred with rich cream, that she had made just for me. My shoulders softened. Breathing carefully, I replaced my mother's face with Sofia's. Her beautiful smile. She was looking right into my eyes, speaking loving words. And it worked, for a moment, at least. I felt a warmth inside my heart.

Then Sofia glanced over her shoulder at something behind her. She turned back to look at me, her brown eyes full of sadness. I felt the familiar sick sorrow rise in my stomach. She had to be going.

On the seventh day I woke up to the sound of birds. One of the windows in the dormitory was open and a cool breeze stirred the curtain. Morning meditation was optional on the final day, so I had slept in. Today we would help clean the monastery and pack our bags. Today we would return to our real lives.

After breakfast, we gathered in the zendo for one final meditation. The silence was suddenly unfamiliar after the chattering of the morning meal. Bright swathes of sunlight fell across the hardwood floor. I tried to follow my breath like a sentinel. Breathing through my mouth, I barely thought of Brad and his feet.

To end the meditation, Roshi Leonard solemnly chimed the bell one last time. Then he told us about The Garden of Great Vows. "I encourage you to add your own," he said. "All are welcome to add their vows. We even have people from around the world who email us and we write them out for them. If you feel moved to, leave a vow yourself."

The garden was surprisingly empty when I arrived. There was still a bit of morning dew on some of the plants. I bent down to rub my face in the lavender. Then I started to reacquaint myself with some of the vows. As I was unrolling a small curl of paper, I heard footsteps, and turned to see Brad.

"Hey," he said.

We hadn't spoken since the silence had been broken, had sat at opposite ends of the long table during breakfast. His energy felt more subdued, although he still had dark bags under his eyes and messy hair.

"Hey," I responded.

"I just packed up the car. We can leave whenever you're ready."

"I'm ready," I said. "Pretty much." I noticed that he was clutching something in his hand. "Do you want some privacy? I've been here a while. I was just leaving."

"That's okay." He shuffled his feet and looked at the ground. "I mean, I was just going to leave something here. For my dad."

"You made a vow for your dad?"

"Sort of. I mean, it's a vow for me, really, but also a vow to him. He's the reason I came here."

"Does he meditate?"

He laughed and shook his head. "No. Not at all. But I promised him I'd stay clean if I came here. It was here or a, you know, a treatment place. But I convinced him here was better. So, I thought I'd leave a vow here. To stay clean for the next year. Until I can come again." He set a folded-up piece of notebook paper on a patch of moss near his feet.

"My father is my mother," he said. "I mean, it was his face I imagined. During that meditation."

"Yeah," I said. "I imagined my ex-partner's face." It was the first time I had said "ex-partner" out loud.

He smiled shyly and shrugged. "We all got someone to be thankful to, I guess."

I looked at his feet. He was wearing his sneakers as shoes again. The bent heels were straightened as much as they could be, and the sneakers were laced up.

He scuffed the ground with one foot and looked around the garden. "I guess we'll be going, then, right?" he asked. "It's a long ride home."

GIRLFRIEND/BOYFRIEND

The problem was that she had always been too good of a listener. With incessant talking, her mother had taught her how to listen. Over coffee, over omelettes, over pancakes with fruit, over dinners of fried vegetables and hamburgers, she heard every story and she listened diligently to every word.

One day on the way to work, she met a boy on the bike path. They were both stopped at a red light and he turned to her, asking her a question and then answering it before she could. Though she could not have explained why, the girl instantly felt drawn to this boy. His jeans were rolled at the cuff, his blond bangs fanned over his hazel eyes. His voice was low and assured, with a barely perceptible undercurrent of uncertainty.

In a week, they were having sex; in two weeks, they had each taken on an appellation, a role that ended with the word "friend." Her period started the third week and she asked him to start using condoms. She hadn't been able to ask before.

She was only eighteen. At seventeen, she had gotten a nose job using money she had saved up for over a year working at her first job, a diner famous for its milkshakes and burgers. She got a nose job, and soon after, she got a boyfriend. She thought these two events were connected and the magazines her mother gave her supported this belief.

Her mother had no friends and for many years had treated her like a younger sister. She was often sitting on the couch in her bathrobe when the girl came home from school or the library. When the temp agency didn't call, her mother sat on the couch all day, eating chips and watching soaps. Or she sat at the kitchen table eating chocolate and reading romances. The apartment was full of paperback Harlequins that the girl would try to organize when her mother was away, stacking them alphabetically in neat piles in the hall. In her first year of high school, she had read some of these novels, but soon found the plots and characters so predictable that she gave up on them. How could all these middle-aged women still be virgins and why were they attracted to men (of course: tall, dark, handsome) who treated them so badly? She turned instead to intriguingly titled books she borrowed from the library.

Gender Trouble. Gender Outlaws. Gender Failure. She felt excited when she saw these dangerous words next to the word "gender." She had, up until shelving the Gender and Sexuality section, considered it a boring, everyday sort of word. In *The Second Sex*—a title all the more alluring for containing the word she had only recently started to use in conversation—she read: "To pose Woman is to pose the absolute Other, without reciprocity, denying against all experience that she is a subject, a fellow human being." She marvelled over the capitalization of "Woman" and "Other." "Truth," too, appeared in capitals, later in the text. She wanted to live a life of truth, or "Truth," although she wasn't sure exactly what she meant by this. She wasn't sure how she felt about "Woman" and she didn't understand what was meant by "Other."

The girl liked her job at the library because she didn't have to listen to anyone. She would plug in her earphones, turn up her music, and start her shift. Some days she craved silence—or the nearest thing, a muffled near-silence—and on those days, she put in earplugs. When patrons asked her questions, she would shrug and point at the reference desk.

While shelving the literature section, she found a book called *Woman Warrior*. An image rose immediately in her mind: a tall, black-haired woman on horseback, wearing protective armour and carrying a sword. She took the book home, hiding it under her coat when she entered the apartment and hiding it under her bed when she wasn't at home.

Reading was one of her few privacies. Reading was not listening. It was deeper. Or, maybe it was a form of listening. But a more solitary, more satisfying form. She decided when to pick up a book or put it down. Some books she left half-finished; others she read to the end. It was up to her when the conversation started, when it stopped.

Her high school reading had consisted mainly of books by dead white men. She read Faulkner, she read Hemingway, she read Whitman. She loved Whitman's "pulse of my nights and days," but the whiny, privileged women in Hemingway made her feel tired and depressed. It was the same feeling she got from being around her mother. The smell of stale chips and old coffee radiated from her mother's couch, along with diet tips, hairstyle suggestions, nosy inquiries about girls she called "sluts," heavy sighs when the girl said she would be out for the night.

After they had been dating for a couple of months, her boyfriend stopped washing his hair regularly. It hung in greasy strands over his eyes, falling in her face, her mouth when they had sex. His room had been near spotless the first time he brought her there to share a warm bottle of Chablis and listen to records. Now it was a body-odoured dumpster, piled with smelly hoodies and bike-greased jeans. It became less and less a place she wanted to be in, or be naked in.

They could have sex at her place; her mother had given her "permission." The very word made her stomach churn, as if in using it ("You have my permission."), her mother was somehow involved in the acts she and her boyfriend performed. She would never have sex with him in that cluttered apartment, her mother coughing just outside her bedroom door or humming merrily while making coffee in the kitchen. She could not think of her mother's erotic life—which was mostly internal at this point she assumed, fuelled by television and Harlequins—without feeling sick. So she tried not to think about it.

While organizing magazines at the library, she came across a spread called "Flip Flop," which featured photos of couples dressed first in their own clothes and then in their partner's. Each couple was comprised of one man and one woman. There were people of various races, but only one older couple. The pictures, the girl supposed, were meant to be humorous: the men squeezed into skirts or shirts they couldn't fully button, their big heels perched atop their partner's small pumps; the women in baggy, rolled up pants and oversized vests, hats slumping over their eyes. While the photographs were interesting to look at, they puzzled the girl. She and her boyfriend dressed pretty much the same: jeans, tee shirts, hoodies, sneakers. They were around the same size, although his tee shirts were a little bit baggy on her.

One young man looked very beautiful in full makeup and his partner's dress, which fit him perfectly. She studied this one for a long time.

For her birthday, her boyfriend got her tickets to a dance performance that had been written up in the local weekly and praised by their artist friends. The performance consisted of five men and five women running and leaping across the stage, sometimes in one large mass, sometimes individually. In parts of the performance, the dancers took off their clothes. The women were repeatedly lifted up and swung around by the men, but none of the women ever lifted the men or each other, even though a few of the men were smaller than the women. In the closing piece, the dancers dressed up: the women in flowing bright dresses and heels, the men in dark suits and ties. The women popped open bottles of champagne and served it in flutes to the men. It was a party scene: as the dancers got progressively more inebriated, they stumbled across the stage. Bottles and glasses were thrown. The performance ended with each male dancer drunkenly cradling a female dancer in his arms, slow dancing as the lights dimmed.

For days after, she thought about this performance, wondering why she felt so angry every time she did. The friends she spoke with had enjoyed it, especially the part where the female dancer held the male dancer's genitals in her hand as he held her genitals in his hand. They found this part very risqué and surprising, and spoke admiringly of the female dancer's well-shaped butt and the male dancer's muscular legs.

"I am not a girl," she told the boy a few nights after the performance, after he had gone down on her and made her cry out. "And I am not sure I will ever be a woman." She rolled on her side and propped her head up with her elbow. The boy covered himself with the sheet and stared at her. For once, he seemed to be at a loss for words. He opened his mouth to speak and then closed it, like a goldfish.

"Okay," he had finally said, combing his hair back from his eyes. "Okay. I'm not really sure about it either. I mean, being a guy. What it means, you know."

"I know," she said, surprised by his answer.

This conversation made her not want to dump him, although she also wanted to dump him. She wanted him to wash his hair. To clean his room. He didn't pay her enough attention, she thought, but then she didn't want someone who dug too deeply into her thoughts, who invaded her privacy.

If only she could get him to quit talking, or to talk less. She liked the way he touched her. Sex seemed to quiet him down. She would lie on top of him afterwards, or he on top of her, and they would breathe a silence together.

But most of the time he wouldn't shut up. He held forth, educating her on things he knew very little about. She imagined him bespectacled, in a tweed blazer with leather elbow patches, smoking a pipe in his study, glowering from behind a lectern. He was always explaining in an authoritative tone he must have inherited from his father. "The interesting thing about the economy is..." he would begin, and her mind would drift off, to the image of herself on a horse, holding up a shield and a sword.

She felt embarrassed for him and she wondered if he ever felt embarrassed for himself. He was like so many boys she had known in school, raising their hands again and again in every class. They always seemed confident that they knew the answers (even though they were often wrong) and perhaps for this reason alone, they were called on more often.

She was one of the silent girls in the back corner, writing in her journal or surreptitiously reading a novel tucked inside her textbook. Even some of her friends, the fearless girls, the ones who painted their nails neon and who had in elementary school lured boys behind the bleachers to beat them up, fell quiet in class when questions were asked. It didn't matter what gender the teacher was—the girls kept their hands down, as if they knew already that their answers wouldn't be the ones the teacher wanted to hear.

Six months into their relationship, the boy's mother calls the boy at work. His father has died. The drunk patriarch. The bitter and intelligent man who thought taking a belt to his son would make him stronger. He keeled over from a heart attack while walking to his car after a boozy business lunch. The boy leaves work and calls her; they go walk by the river.

"I'm sorry" is all she can think to say.

"Why? Did you kill him?"

It takes her a few seconds to realize he is joking. She looks at his face. It is whiter than usual.

"I once saw a dead body floating down here," he says.

"When?"

He shrugs. "A long time ago." He pauses. "Yeah, the guy was really dead, though."

"But he wasn't your father."

He looks at her angrily. "Why did you say that?"

She looks away, at a crow pulling fast food wrappers out of a garbage can. A few office workers sit on benches eating their lunches. A couple of college students are making out on a blanket. Embarrassment rises in her. She knows it was a cruel thing to say. "I don't know." Her face feels hot. "To get a reaction, I guess. I'm sorry."

"Whatever." He starts to walk quickly, as if he might leave her behind. But after a few steps, he slows, and lets her catch up. They walk in silence, the river flowing next to them like a fat brown snake. Logs loosed from lumber barges float next to bits of trash and bottles glinting in the sun.

His head is down, his hands in his jean pockets. She knows she should be more careful with him. She should stroke the back of his neck and offer to make him soup or something. She should take him out to a funny or scary movie. But instead, she finds herself saying, "I'm never going to cook for you."

He looks up from the ground, his eyes red and tired. "Why are you saying this shit?"

"I'm just saying that I'm not just some girl you can take on dates and not take seriously."

This appears to take him by surprise. He brushes his hair out of his eyes. "What are you talking about?"

"You don't listen to me. You think I'm just some stupid girl."

"What are you talking about? Seriously. No one sees women that way anymore."

"Then why do you always interrupt me?"

"Why do I—?"

"Interrupt me. Finish my sentences. Assume you know what I'm going to say before I say it."

"Do we have to talk about this now?"

"Yes."

"I feel like shit."

"So do I."

He lets out a long sigh and looks out across the river at a kayaker paddling toward the other shore. His shoulders hunch forward. In his black tee shirt and hoodie, he looks out of place next to the bright pots of begonias and marigolds that line the path. "You're so quiet all the time. You never even talk practically. This is the most you've ever said really. I mean really talked about stuff."

"You never give me a chance."

He turns toward her abruptly. "Maybe you should just give *me* a chance. To be myself. Give me a break instead of criticizing me. When my dad just died."

"Does 'being yourself' mean never listening? Never thinking about me? Never thinking and never fucking listening?" She knows her voice is rising, but she feels like she can't control it. The anger is in her, a coursing river, the blood hot in her ears, blooming behind her cheeks. She looks around. A suited woman on a bench folds up a napkin and dabs the corners of her mouth. Behind her, the couple on the blanket wrestle and screech with laughter.

She knows it is not the right time, the right place. But she has been holding this conversation in her chest for so many weeks now.

He looks at the ground. His lips quiver. She has never seen him cry. She did not realize until this moment that she has been wanting to.

Again she sees herself on the horse. She remembers the books beneath her bed, their bright covers, red and royal blue. Their bold titles in gold and silver letters, loud as the sound of her boots when she strides into the library. She thinks of how good it feels to walk with purpose, to have a place to go. To be surrounded by the smell of new books, of glue and paper and ink. To be away from the stale smell of her mother's bathrobe, her unkempt hair, the stacks of romance novels next to her bed.

This boy is only a little bit tall and only marginally handsome. His hair is not dark. His voice isn't very deep. His father is dead. He is looking at her now and he is about to ask her something.

DINNER PARTY

"The kids are still up. We couldn't get them to go to bed early. At least they're upstairs. They're crazy on sugar." Sandra's orange hair billows out around her handsome face. She clutches a glass of whisky in one hand, ice cubes melting, and holds out the other arm to hug us. Wide gold bracelets slip down toward her elbows. She's wearing a low-cut white blouse and the edge of her pink bra peeks out. As she clutches us, I smell her perfume, musky and foresty.

I look over her shoulder at the living room strewn with Barbie dolls, trucks and cars, crayons, paper, scissors, children's clothing. The chairs and couch are pushed together, blankets draped over them.

Sandra leads us inside. "Celia was making a fort. And Betsy won't play with her, so guess who gets to?" She points to herself.

From the kitchen Bert calls, "Hey ho! Who wants a drink?"

Roxanne is already at the doorway of the kitchen to greet him. She grabs him in a long hug.

Bert is wearing a large white chef's apron streaked with tomato sauce. He carefully balances a full glass of red wine against Roxanne's back as he embraces her.

"Strangers," he says. "Welcome back to our home."

The kitchen table is covered with encrusted cereal bowls and orange juice glasses from breakfast. Children's finger paintings and crayon drawings are taped to the walls and held to the fridge with magnets. An open can of tomato sauce and a chunk of broccoli sit on the kitchen counter next to a stack of dirty plates. The patio doors are open and a lilac breeze stirs the air.

"A drink?" Bert offers. "We'll join you. I poured half a bottle down my throat the minute I walked into the house."

I rarely drink anymore. Beer makes me nauseous and wine gives me a headache. Cider makes my ears itch. I tell mean lies when on tequila and the last time I drank vodka I woke up on the bathroom floor. "I'll have a little lime with soda water, if you have it," I say.

"Wine for me, thanks," Roxanne says, touching Bert's arm.

Roxanne and Bert went to university together in Ontario. They dated for a couple of months during second year, until Rox discovered she was a lesbian. Bert was devastated, although within weeks he started dating her best friend, who he called "the prettier one." Out of this unlikely beginning, they built a friendship that followed them across provinces and through years.

"I'll have a refill," says Sandra, downing the whisky in her glass and setting it on the counter. She smiles at me. Her cheeks are a little flushed; her eyes are bright and appear slightly wet.

A shrieking starts, followed by pounding footsteps. Celia and Betsy burst into the kitchen. I haven't seen them in about a year and their hair is redder, longer. They are maybe two years apart, both long-limbed and freckled.

"She's gross! Mom! You won't believe it!" yells Betsy, the older one.

"I didn't!" Celia pushes her sister against the counter. "You're gross. I hate you!"

"She put Barbie's legs in her you-know-what!" Betsy crows triumphantly.

Bert hands Roxanne a glass of wine and slips a tumbler of soda water into my hand. He turns back to his sauce and pointedly whistles while stirring. "Don't you two have somewhere to be right now?" he says. "Like upstairs? Like watching TV? Like not bothering us? I thought we had a deal."

"You're a sick sicko," Betsy says. "I'm not going back up there," she says to her parents. She crosses her arms and pouts.

Sandra takes an ice cube tray out of the freezer and drops a couple of cubes into her glass. "I think you'd better listen to your father on this one," she says, pouring soda water and then whisky into her glass. She slides over and tips the whisky bottle over my glass, spilling some in before I have a chance to object. "I'd listen to him if I were you."

When Sandra comes back downstairs, her face is red and her hair stands up like static around her head. "Well, that was a project," she said. "After I convinced Celia it wasn't a good idea to brush Barbie's crotch with her toothbrush, I had to convince Betsy to sleep in her bed rather than ours. It's funny—last week Celia saw some of my underwear hanging in the bathroom and asked if I had hurt myself. I had to explain the whole period thing to her right there and then. She's only six."

I look into my glass. Roxanne and I have been talking about having children. After five years, I feel it's time, but Rox isn't there yet.

Roxanne is standing close to Bert as he stirs the tomato sauce. Her hand is on his back and they are talking in low tones. Roxanne laughs at something and takes a big sip from her glass.

Sandra asks me if I want to go outside to look at the flowers. She takes a pack of cigarettes out of her purse. "I quit, but then I started again."

It's still light out, although dusk is fast approaching. Out the patio doors next to the lilac is a huge rhododendron with garish pink flowers like children's tutus.

We sit on rusty lawn chairs wedged into parched grass. Sandra smiles and waves the whisky bottle in my direction. I cover the mouth of my glass. There is something wet and hungry in her gaze.

She sets the bottle down on a rickety table and lights a ciga-rette. "I don't judge people anymore," she says. "I understand why people cheat. I understand why they have affairs. I know why people are alcoholics. I understand." She sips from her drink. "Bert and I have been thinking. Yoga teacher training. Open a studio. What do you think? There's this guy in Mexico, this guru or something, who does trainings over Christmas and New

Year's. We can leave the kids with my parents and go become yogis. And then start our own place. What do you think?"

I don't know what to say. I am trying not to peer into the kitchen, at Roxanne leaning on Bert. I'm trying not to think about what she might do tonight, how far she'll go. I'm trying, especially, not to remember that the last time she saw Bert, at some fundraiser of Sandra's, was the last time she wanted to have sex with me. She came home late, drunk to the bones, and practically tore my clothes off. She made me turn the lights out and wear the biggest cock. It had been hot at the time, but the next morning she had left early for work and I was lonely as I made my morning coffee. I search my brain for something to say. "In this neighbourhood?"

She drags on her cigarette. "No, no, in Mexico. He has a whole centre or something. Our friends went and had a great time. He's enlightened, or almost. He's the real deal. It's only two thousand each and then you're certified. Our friends came back so skinny and tanned and so...you know, calm. I couldn't believe it. She's a divorce lawyer, for God's sake. They don't want to open a place, but they said if we did, they'd teach for us. Or at least come to our classes. It's just an idea but we're really considering it."

"Rox and I are considering having a kid," I blurt out. Which isn't exactly accurate. What we've actually been doing is fighting about it.

"A kid?" She looks surprised, but then quickly recovers. "How exciting! I'm sure you'll be great parents."

I look through the patio doors into the kitchen. Roxanne and Bert are still standing close to each other at the stove. Bert lifts up the wooden spoon to give her a taste of the sauce. I look back down at my drink. I've barely made a dent in it.

"Rox isn't that into it, to tell you the truth. But I'd like to start soon. I'm not getting any younger."

"She probably doesn't want to ruin her figure," Sandra jokes.

"She won't. I'll carry."

"You?" This time it takes her a minute to regain her composure. "I mean, you don't seem like the type. I mean—"

"It's okay," I interrupt. "A lot of people assume. I guess because Rox wears dresses and I don't." I try to rescue Sandra with a joke, but it falls flat.

"Oh, I didn't assume that, it's just that…" She trails off, looking down at the ground. Then she grinds out her cigarette in a jar lid perched on the table and dumps more whisky into her glass. This time, she doesn't offer me any.

Into this uncomfortable silence steps Roxanne, flushed and beaming. "Guess what?" She rests her hand on the back of my neck, then quickly takes it away as if thinking better of it. "Bert just invited me to go to this yoga teachers' training in Mexico. Doesn't that sound fabulous?"

I look at Sandra. She smiles blithely and takes a sip of her drink.

"I don't know if we can afford it right now," I say. "We have some big expenses coming up." I mean the baby, but Roxanne— either intentionally or obliviously—doesn't clue in.

"We've got all that savings. Besides, it will be good for me. I need a break. Things have been so stressful lately. Yoga!" She throws up her hands dramatically. I'm not sure who she is performing for.

Sandra gets up. "I'd better check on that sauce, make sure Bert isn't fucking it up." She smiles.

We're left alone, and I feel, as I often have lately, that we don't know what to say to each other.

Rox looks defiant. She sits down in Sandra's chair and pulls a cigarette out of the pack Sandra forgot to take with her. She lights it and leans back, crossing her legs. Her red dress rides up her thighs. "You've got to quit trying to control me," she says, using a tone she might use to tell me what to add to a grocery list. "I'm tired of it. I'm tired of all this..." She holds her hand up, as if the words she is looking for will fall from the sky and land in her palm. She takes a drag and blows smoke over her shoulder.

"You're attracted to him," I say flatly.

"I'm attracted to *life*." Her tone is accusatory.

"I'm not life, I guess." My voice sounds pathetic even to me.

"You're just...you're just..." She pauses for a moment. "You're just you." Why does this sound so definite, so much like a final judgment?

Bert calls jovially from the kitchen, "Dinner's up, crew! Come and get it!"

I don't know if I've ever felt less hungry. I stare down into my unfinished drink. Rox rises to her feet and shakes out her dress. Her face looks both pissed off and resigned. I wonder how I look to her, and then I realize that this thought makes me feel afraid.

"We're ready," she says, as she strides toward the open door, toward the smell of garlic and oregano. "We're right here."

THE SHAPE

She sips and rocks and thinks. A glass, encrusted with the silty residue of days of red wine, clutched in her hand. Her thick white hair has been thinning these last few weeks; wisps of hair cover the shoulders of her black sweater, as if a fluffy white cat had perched there and then departed, leaving its snowy fur.

The days are very short now. The windows suddenly black, then pink with dawn. She closes her eyes to nap and opens them to blue light seeping into the room. Her chair is by the window so she can see out, but a gnarled old fig tree blocks her view of the street. She can hear children yelling at play and her neighbours arguing about real estate on their front porch. She hears people trying to be surreptitious as they steal her figs, although one time a young man's loud voice abruptly wakes her: "Bring the ladder over here!"

The figs are ripe. The birds devour them. The fruit falls to the ground, splits open, releasing a sweet smell that turns to rot. They smear the stairs, the walk, with seedy muck. She hates figs. Their gooey insides, their too strong, too sweet taste. Yet she used to love eating them. Now she can't imagine eating anything.

The figs are ripe. That means it's summer. She is certain now. Summer. Summer again.

Something glimmers in the corner of the room. A light-shape in a dress-like garment. A robe?

She is not afraid or surprised. The starvation diet and the wine keep her from being afraid of anything.

She might be hallucinating. Like the time her eldest son— long dead from a motorcycle crash—visited her. He held his helmet under one arm and brushed his long, brown hair back from his face before leaning in to kiss her cheek. He smelled like cigarettes and motorcycle grease and some woodsy soap. She knew he had come to talk to her about *Open Secrets,* the book of stories she had sent him, and she hoped she remembered enough about the plots and characters to engage in a worthwhile discussion. She did not want to waste his time with her forgetfulness.

It could be a hallucination. There was the time she fell and couldn't get up from the floor for ten hours and finally saw a gentle, masculine hand reaching out from the arm of a blue robe to help her—Jesus? Although she didn't believe in him. One of her daughters had found her the next day and hadn't believed her when she shared her vision.

The light-shape shimmers, as if this shimmering is a form of speech. The old woman takes another sip of her wine and blinks.

Now the shape appears to be a big, white fluffy cat. It purrs, then arches its back and hisses, its eyes a cold black. Even through the dulling wine, the old woman feels something akin to fear. Her hands, which always shake now, clench like frozen claws.

"What are you?" she croaks.

The shape throbs with light and returns to its original form, a human-ish blur in an incandescent robe or dress.

"I'm the hospital," the shape says.

"The what?"

"The hospital."

"You're a ghost!" the old woman says angrily, as if she has just found out something that was being hidden from her. She thumps her glass down on the table. "That's what you are."

The shape sighs. A thousand tremulous lights shuddering. Then silence.

The old woman takes a different tack. She dusts off her most polite voice. "What I meant to ask was, who are you? I mean, my dead son visited me once so I know that's possible, and more recently a hand reached out..."

She stops because the shape is shaking again, this time quite vehemently. It is laughing! She is being laughed at by a ghost!

"What's so funny?" she snaps.

There is a shifting of light in the area of what might be the face. Is the shape smiling? "Isn't it time for you to go to the hospital?" the kindly voice asks. "Your children are worried. You haven't been answering their calls."

The old woman feels something flutter in her stomach, a sort of muffled panic. Does she have any children? She remembers most clearly the dead son. But were there others?

"Your daughter stopped by with groceries and you hid behind the curtains," the shape calmly tells her.

Now the old woman remembers. She heard the neighbours talking on their porch. They said she had twelve children. Or was it thirteen? But were they children, or just unlucky numbers, one after another? Their births—one with an umbilical cord wrapped around her neck, blue-skinned like a saint, and always so sensitive after that, the quickest to tears. The colicky one who wouldn't stop screaming. And the quiet ones who laid so still in their cribs, staring at the ceiling with impassive brown eyes.

But those were all nightmares! Not her real children, the ones who never visit her, never call. All twelve of them. Or thirteen?

The shape throbs again, sympathetically, it seems to her. She feels it reaching across the room to her in a sort of embrace. Then it lightens, disappears.

She is alone again. She looks around the room, at the peeling paint, the dust piled in the corners. She sips her wine. She rocks. The chair's creaking is a comfort because it is not silence. Outside it is still summer, she thinks. She is sure there are figs on the tree. She would like to get up from her chair now and go pick one. But it is too far. She sleeps.

When she wakes, it is still daylight. Morning, she thinks. Morning again. She vaguely remembers talking to someone. Who? Had someone visited her?

The light is fresh. It brightens the smears on her wineglass. She sees her hands shake as she lifts it from the table. It is normal for her hands to shake. She is old. She knows this, but it has been some time since she could bear to look in the mirror. Her skin is cracked, a ghostly red-veined paper loosely covering the face of a skeleton.

The last time she was in the hospital they gave her bigger and bigger pills, and only a few sips of water. Some of the pills she choked on. The physical therapists, the speech therapists, the nurses—perky, young, convinced of her ability to heal—urged her to clomp up and down the hall with her walker, to practice sitting up, rolling to her side, and getting out of bed. She hated these exercises, but complied.

No one visited her and she had to let these smiling strangers help her in the bathroom. She had no privacy. She would lie in bed, breathing in the scents of floor wax and medicine, listening to the squeaks of food carts and nurses' shoes in the hall, and she would silently curse them.

She shared the room with four others, and during the week she stayed there, two of them died. The two who lived had throngs of visitors, friends with daisies, oranges, fat shiny gift shop novels; relatives who sang songs and stayed until two or three in the morning, whispering to each other. There was always a sister or adult grandchild to hold their hands, spoon feed them homemade applesauce or yogurt from the hospital tray.

At first an annoyance, their murmurs, after a time, soothed her—this was the code of people who understood each other, who shared an intimacy.

Late at night, she would lay on her back and imagine turning over on her side, using the bars to hoist herself up. She did the exercises over and over in her mind. She knew she must keep doing them. She must get stronger; she would get stronger. And once she was strong enough, she would be released.

AFTER HALLOWEEN

She is coming down the stairs in her tall, tall boots. She is walking slowly, not meeting my eyes. Her hair is a frizzy red halo; her lips look burnt.

Outside the dogs are crying. They always howl this time of year. The moon cackles. It is impossible to find my laughter.

"I'm going," she says, slinging a small gold purse over her shoulder.

"That's all?" I ask.

"All what?"

"All you're bringing with you?"

"Oh." She airily waves her hand. "I don't need any of this."

This is simply the contents of the small one-bedroom we've been sharing for two years. I glance around at the worn blue couch, the potted aloes, then stare out the cracked window, hoping to see one of the dogs. I think the moon is smirking now, but can't be sure.

"Bye lover." She holds out her cheek for a kiss.

I lean for her lips. She turns her head and laughs, patting my arm.

After she's gone, a silence settles over the apartment. The dogs must be asleep. I notice that all the pictures on the walls are askew. A letter from one of our mothers flutters on the coffee table next to a bowl of apples.

I remember the day, so many years ago, that my mother brought home a limping dog. The whimpering as my mother bathed its wounds. It was fall, turning to winter. Dim lamps in windows, shadowy streets filling me with wonder. I had always loved hinges—the places where death and birth meet. Orange-brown leaves rotting in a puddle as snow begins to fall, waking at dawn on an overnight train. I always knew I would pack up this place alone.

The pale green apples glow in the wooden bowl like so many moons. Soon I will wash the windows. I will wash the cupboards; I will wash the floors. I will wash the mirror that once held us and I will wash and wash my face.

HIDE AND SEEK

The old woman told young George to come visit early. To leave his shoes and mat in his room. To walk to her slowly, through the high grass, along the dirt path, and to listen to what the trees were saying on the way.

"What did you hear?" she demanded the moment he entered her cabin.

But he hadn't heard a thing.

Most of the time, the old woman sat in her cabin on an embroidered orange cushion made for her by one of her devotees. She sat on this cushion and she did her "work."

Was it praying? he wanted to know.

"No, not praying," she replied. "I am feeling everything and with a sort of thinking I am moulding what is needed. At times it is more painful than you or almost anyone could imagine, but even if the pain is so strong that it pulls my left arm out of my socket, my right arm is anchored in an unfathomable bliss."

Are you ever torn in two? he wanted to know.

And she laughed and watched an ant crawl along the hem of her robe.

Each day she took a walk for one or two hours. Sometimes she walked alone. Sometimes she invited George to walk with her. They walked under the hot sun and under shielding trees, through tall fields of dry grass and patches of low, scrubby bushes. On their first walk together, the old woman told him, "Georgie, I cannot tell this to many of my visitors because they will not understand and their feelings will be hurt. But I will tell you, since you are going to stay here a while. Listen to me carefully: There is absolutely nothing I want to say and absolutely nothing I want to hear. So if you have an itch to speak, make sure you feel deep inside yourself and speak from your most sincere place."

After this, George did not talk for three days. He took two silent walks with the old woman and watched the white moths and yellow butterflies cavort through the wildflowers and tried to listen to their language as she had instructed.

On the fourth day, he could not contain himself. As he left the old woman to head back to his cabin, a question burbled from his lips. "Should I write poems? I've been writing poems. In my head."

The old woman smiled. "Come visit me after dinner."

Later that evening George found her rocking in a rocking chair a devotee had recently built for her, on the front porch that had been added to her cabin the week before. She had the book of a famous mystical poet, many centuries dead, open on her lap. As usual, her face bore a calm smile. Her long white hair was pulled back in a ponytail and her eyes were two bright blue worlds. She nodded as George climbed up to the porch.

George took this as a signal that he should start reciting his poems. He opened his mouth to begin, but the old woman held up her hand and signalled for him to wait. Then she started to speak. "For years, Georgie, I walked. I walked back and forth across this country, through cities, through meadows, down highways, and up small country roads. When I was tired, I curled up by the side of the road and slept. Strangers gave me food and water and clothing when it got too cold. I carried with me only a pad of paper and a pen, to write messages to those I encountered, for at that time, I did not speak. I owned no comb. My hair was a rat's nest. But I usually found some sort of stream or lake in which to wash my clothes, and so I stayed fairly clean.

"People often offered me rides, but I always refused. Walking was my prayer. I had to keep walking.

"Then one day, after ten or fifteen years, a kind lady with a bushel of apples and two big dogs in the back of her truck asked me if I'd like a ride into town. And instead of smiling and shaking my head, I heard a voice coming out of my mouth, a voice I had not heard in some time, say, 'Yes, thank you.' And I climbed into her truck and she brought me here and asked me to stay. And that's how this centre was built."

George had heard this story before, but it was different hearing it from the old woman's own mouth. He marvelled at the good fortune of the farmer who had picked her up. This woman with apples and dogs he had never met, as she had died some years before he came to the centre, but he still envied her incredible luck—to have a living saint camped out in your own backyard, to have a spiritual centre sprout up next to your backdoor—all from just picking up an old woman on a dusty country road!

George looked at the old woman's tanned and lined face as she rocked in her chair, head bent toward her hands folded in her lap. He wondered if now was the time for him to start reciting his poems. He cleared his throat. The old woman looked up at him and smiled. "That's all for today, Georgie."

Although she had told him on their first walk that she had nothing left to say, George noticed that the old woman often talked to him at length about her experiences. Sometimes she would call for him to come to her cabin in the evening, and, as she rocked in her chair, she would tell him two or three stories, all from her years of searching. He would sit at the top of the stairs and listen, but his listening was not profound. He often thought of stories from his own life that he would like to share, and on occasion, he tried to tell her how he had worked for his father's insurance company, how bored he had been of television as a child, how he had loved to go into the woods alone with his dog. But whenever he'd start to speak, she would interrupt him.

"Don't speak, Georgie. Just be."

Sometimes he would try to object and she would quietly, kindly reprimand him. "No, George. Don't speak. Listen. *Listen*. Have you heard what the birds are telling you today?"

And he would have to admit that he had heard nothing of the birds all day, hadn't even paid attention to their constant song, their flitting in the trees outside his window.

After some weeks of this, he was very frustrated. He had hitch-hiked from a large eastern city with only a small backpack and the address of the centre written on a torn piece of envelope. His friends had thought he was losing his mind. He had given up his apartment, his job, his phone, his life—all to study with her. But all she did was lecture him and silence him when he tried to speak. Her teachings did not seem very useful. They were mostly anecdotes about her walking travels. Why was he here? This was not the life, the truth he was seeking.

On the day he decided he would roll up his mat and blanket and pack his three shirts, the old woman summoned him to her cabin. He did not see her rocking on the porch as he approached, but he heard laughter and shuffling behind the cabin. As he peeked around, he saw her playing marbles in the dust with two of her devotees, a young man and a young woman, both dressed in white. She looked up as he approached.

"Georgie! There you are!"

The devotees rolled the marbles under the cabin and flitted away like moths. The old woman straightened from her crouch and approached George.

"Come inside," she said. "I have something for you."

He followed her into the cabin. She poked around, lifting up blankets and pillows and looking under them until she found what she was looking for: a small red notebook. She sat down on her orange cushion and opened it. She leafed through the first few pages, which were covered with unintelligible handwriting, pausing here and there to silently read a few passages, mouthing the words as she did. Then she looked up at George and smiled as she started ripping out the pages, one by one, crumpling them into little balls at her feet. When she had torn out all of the written-on pages, she handed George the blank book.

So he decided to stay. Each day he got up before dawn and splashed his face with cold water from the faucet outside his cabin. Then he went inside and did a few stretches he had learned from one of the old woman's devotees. After that, he rolled up his sleeping mat and made a little cushion on which he sat, trying to follow his breath and banish thoughts from his head. He could never stop his thoughts and he often lost track of his breath, and after a time, he decided that was enough and got up from his mat and took out the notebook and began to write.

The words came out haltingly and they often didn't make sense to him. One word would follow another in an order he didn't understand. He used words he never had used in conversation, words he didn't even know the meaning of. He felt that he was writing down thoughts which weren't his own. He was often afraid of the lines he wrote, and could seldom bring himself to reread them.

After a couple of weeks, the old woman summoned him to

her cabin one morning. As usual, she was rocking on her porch, dressed completely in white. Her hair was covered with a white cloth. A pot of ginger tea steamed on a log table next to her chair, two small cups next to it. She rolled two blue marbles together in one of her palms.

"So you've been working hard," she said.

He nodded, clutching the notebook. It was as if his hands belonged to someone else, but he knew it was his own sweat running down his palms.

She smiled encouragingly. "Let's hear them, then."

He swallowed, but couldn't speak. After an awkward moment, he mutely handed her the notebook.

She took it from him, opened it, and then immediately shut it and handed it back to him. She shook her head and motioned for him to leave.

He went back to his cabin in deep despair. Why had he come here? Why was he writing? *What* was he writing? Why, when he had finally been invited to sound his voice, had he faltered?

He paced the cabin all day, twisting his hands together and pulling at his hair. When he lay down on his mat at nightfall, he was sure he wouldn't be able to sleep. But he immediately dropped into a deep slumber.

The next day he woke up and went through his morning routine. But when he reached for his notebook next to his mat, it wasn't there. He searched his entire cabin, rolling and unrolling his mat, shaking out his blanket. His pen rested on the window ledge where he kept it, but his notebook was nowhere to be found.

He was furious. Had one of her devotees stolen it? They were sneaky, quiet people who dressed only in white and padded around silently in hand-sewn slippers, bringing bowls of soup and smiling too much. Sure, one had taught him some stretches, and they seemed nice enough, but he wouldn't be surprised if there was more than one thief among them. The old woman would be blind to any shortcomings, he was sure—she treated them like her own precious children, and could often be seen laughing with them, rolling marbles in the dust or playing hopscotch with a few small sticks.

Before he could continue these thoughts, there was a knock on the door. He opened it to find a young man in a white dress smiling and gesturing for George to follow him. George resisted the urge to slam the door in his face. He held up his index finger to signal "just a moment," and then carefully shut the door. He closed his eyes and counted five in and five out breaths. Then he opened his eyes and looked around the room. The notebook was still nowhere to be seen.

He opened the door again and started to follow the young man, who was already walking away from his cabin. On the path leading up to the old woman's porch, the young man suddenly veered off and started walking across a field of tall grass. After about ten feet, he halted abruptly, signalling to George to come close to him. He then pointed to a stand of birch trees many yards away. He smiled at George, nodded his head and then turned to walk back toward the path.

George looked at the stand of trees, and then looked around. Where was the old woman? Meditating under a tree? That was unlike her, as she usually meditated in her cabin. Not that she called it meditating.

He started to walk slowly across the field, brushing the tips of the grass with his fingers. It was a large field, with wildflowers growing in sporadic clumps. Yellow and orange butterflies flitted about in the sun. Every few steps, he stumbled on a stone or some knot in the grass. There was the smell of dry hay and pollen.

He was getting closer to the trees, but he still didn't see the old woman. She wasn't sitting under a tree and she was not standing beside one. He grew more puzzled with each step. Why had he been brought here? What did she want? To wave his notebook of ridiculous scribbles in front of his face and laugh? To banish him from this place for refusing to read them to her? Had she sensed his jealous thoughts about her devoted pupils, the accusations and judgments he had made in his mind? Perhaps she knew he had masturbated. But that was weeks ago, and it had only been once. Why was she calling him now?

He heard a slithering sound near his foot and startled. A snake? Then he heard the old woman's laughter behind him. He whirled around. But only the tall blank grass and purple and red wildflowers greeted him. He looked back at the stand of trees. A bit of white cloth drifted out from behind one of the trunks. There she was! Hiding behind a tree. He should have known. She loved games. He had never been invited to play with her and her devotees, but today it seemed she was finally engaging him in a game of hide and seek. He felt like running towards her and grabbing her robe like a child, yelling, "I got you! You're it! You're it!" But what if it wasn't a game after all? Then he would again be making a fool of himself. Better not to run. He forced himself to walk slowly, listening for snakes so he could jump before being bitten.

When he got closer, he saw that what he had thought was the old woman's robe was just a piece of white cloth caught on a branch, twirling in the breeze. He took it in his hand, feeling its smooth texture and warmth. Again, he heard the laughter behind him. He turned quickly. She was standing there, in the shadiest part of the grove. Although, "standing" wasn't the correct word. Her feet weren't touching the ground. She was floating.

He took a few steps closer. He couldn't believe what he was seeing. Her devotees told tales of her powers, but George had never seen anything and he wasn't sure he believed them. The old woman herself had said that he would never see her perform any feats of magic. "I don't believe in it," she had said, matter-of-factly. "Tricks are for magicians on stages who pull bunnies out of hats. Believe me or don't, but I won't fly for you or raise the dead."

But there she was. Levitating!

And there was something in her hand. His notebook.

He looked at her face, lined with wrinkles and glowing as if lit from within by a candle. Her eyes were bright and youthful, but also deeply wise, as if she was a newborn who already knew everything. She smiled at him mischievously. "It's time for you to go home, Georgie," she said. "Go home and get married. Work with your hands. Carpentry, construction—open a bakery. Have some children. Go home, now." Then she lifted one arm and hurled the notebook at him.

It struck him hard on the chest and fell to the ground. He was too stunned to speak. The leaves fluttered above and the birds sang in the branches. He was certain their trilling had never been so loud or so clear. He looked down at the red notebook splayed on the dirt. When he looked back up, the old woman was gone. The piece of cloth that had been caught on the tree was also gone. And in his chest this incredible pain. He picked up the notebook and walked slowly back to his cabin.

In his cabin, his mat and blanket were already rolled up and tied with a rope. His few shirts were folded neatly in his backpack.

Seeing this, he felt such anguish that he dropped to his knees and fell forward, clutching the notebook to his chest. His forehead touched the floor and he fell instantly into a dead sleep.

He woke with a start to the sound of an old woman's laughter. He was lying in a field of tall grass, a damp notebook under his head. A breeze moved the grasses above him; they seemed to breathe. The air smelled like wet hay and flowers on the verge of rot. His chest felt bruised, as if he had been kicked by someone wearing heavy boots. He felt that he had been living with this ache for a very long time, perhaps his whole life.

He had been dreaming of a boy holding his hand as they climbed stairs, a wild-haired girl racing to a gold merry-go-round. Beautiful, blue-eyed children who called him "Papa." The beautiful children he never had.

He wasn't sure if the damp on his notebook was from the dew

or from someone's—his own?—tears. Where was he? And why was he here?

His limbs ached. He touched his face and head, and felt long, coarse hair, a long beard he knew was white. The moon was full above him, and very bright. It shone a cold light.

MIDNIGHT

Some weird angels showed up. They were weird angels because they didn't look like angels. They looked like devils. But Johanna knew they were angels.

One with short, curly blond hair and pink eyes put a record on. Punk?

Jazz.

Two of the angels started to dance, slowly, out of sync with the music.

Johanna sat up on the couch; her favourite yellow blanket slipped to the floor. She slept on the couch because her bed had started to give her nightmares. She was so sick of all these divine presences. Maybe she had taken too many vitamins the night before. Or maybe it was all the holy books she'd been burning.

"I read them before I burn them," she explained vaguely.

"You'd better call your mother," the curly angel said.

"If I had a mother, I'd call her *right now*," Johanna replied.

"That's what I said." Curly handed her the phone. "Call your mother."

Johanna heard the hiss of the burner as one of the other angels put the coffee on. The dancing angels were now using her kitchen towels to polish their short horns.

Her apartment seemed like hell. But Johanna knew it was heaven. She started dialling.

THE MAGICIAN

5 a.m.—the dregs of the party. A few rockers doing bong hits in the kitchen, two sparkle-shirted sisters holding each other up and puking over the back porch railing, slumped figures on the floor, a heavy stench of smoke and beer. Trance music pulsed from one of the upstairs bedrooms. Angela's very high girlfriend Jake was in an achingly long philosophical conversation with a woman who wore a chain linking her lip, nose, and ear piercings. Angela kissed Jake on the cheek and slipped out.

The street sparkled with ice and the remnants of midnight. Angela loved walking at night, especially in winter. The air so cold it singed the hair in her nostrils, the tree branches a broken calligraphy against the sky, the moon whitely grinning, or opening its mouth wide to *aaahhh*, to sing. The silence of the empty streets.

She was surprisingly sober. It had been hours since she had finished her share of the gin—it had left her clear-eyed and thoughtful. She would walk and think.

It was a cold two miles to her apartment. The wind was mercifully at her back, pushing her forward. She had left her gloves at the party but her scarf warmed her neck and her wool hat was like the reassuring hand of a grandmother. She buried her hands into the pockets of her long black coat. The wind felt like it might lift her up like a witch on a broom. A witch on a broom. Where had that myth come from? Fear of sweeping, of "women's work"? Brooms to sweep spirits out of the house? Cleanliness close to godliness? But witches weren't thought of as "godly"... Angela remembered her grandmother singing to herself as she swept the kitchen, telling her it was bad luck to leave the broom lying on the floor or propped upside down in the closet. But riding the broom like a horse—was the broom a phallus, then? A very long dildo, a cock without a man...

Steeped in these thoughts, she didn't notice the man jaywalking, trying to cross his path with hers, until he was suddenly in her periphery, a dark figure limping quickly towards her. Then he was in front of her, white face glowing, thin black moustache quivering over thin lips, watery, seeking eyes.

At first Angela did not recognize him. She assumed he was one of the addicts who lived in the falling-down Victorians on this string of drug blocks. Then the streetlight caught his cheekbones, turning the rest of his face to shadow, and she remembered the black top hat he had been wearing at the party. Without it, his black hair whipped in the wind. His eyes were light blue and he seemed to have difficulty focusing. He acted (was he acting?) as if he didn't recognize her.

"Got a smoke? So cold out here. A smoke?" He was shivering

in his thin layers of black and purple clothing. His jacket had a huge rip down the sleeve, from the shoulder to the elbow. She wondered if he had been in a fight since he'd left the party.

At the party, he had been in every room she entered, trying to commandeer the attention of everyone with tricks involving cards or coins and glasses of water. In one of the upstairs bedrooms where she had left her coat, she found him surrounded by a small, very stoned audience as he spread tarot cards out on the bed, a silver ring flashing on each finger. Later, she came into the kitchen to refill her drink and heard him attempting to regale a beautiful, red-headed trans woman with a series of dead baby jokes. He told them hurriedly, one after another, as if doing a stand-up routine: "What is the difference between a pile of dead babies and a pile of bowling balls? What is the difference between a Cadillac and a pile of dead babies?" She fumbled with the gin, spilling some on the counter as she tried to get out of the kitchen as fast as she could. As she was leaving, he started on the pedophile jokes.

Now this—there was no other way to put it—character was in front of her. It was as if he had stepped out of some movie she never managed to watch during her teenage years, some bad young adult novel about first love and vampires. He wore a garland of long necklaces, some with skulls and daggers, some with beads and fake diamonds. At the corner of his mouth a cold sore festered. His eyes kept trying to meet hers and kept failing. He seemed to be glancing up at the branches above her head or over her shoulder at some ghost.

She felt an anger growing in her. Here he was. In her way.

Blocking her path. He felt free to interrupt her walk, her time alone, away from Jake, away from the party drunks. This was one of the few holy spaces left for her in the entire world. And he was trying to ruin that.

"No, I don't have a smoke," she said coldly. She felt like she was pulling the ice out of every tree branch, out of every ragged blade of grass, off of every pane of glass in every frozen window and directing it into his watery blue eyes. It was a trick her grandmother had taught her. Most of her grandmother's tricks she didn't remember, but there were a few she still used. This one—her grandmother called it "the frigid gaze"—had worked for her many times. She hoped it would work for her now.

The magician—as she had decided to call him—shrugged and shifted, then clutched his arms. She realized in that moment that he had no plan, but would probably try to hurt her if he could. The pathetic shivering was part of his act. Or was it? He was alone; he had obviously not scored at the party as he hoped. None of his tricks had worked. Despite the black jeans hugging his slender thighs and the wave of hair falling over his eyes like a crow's wing, he had not managed to woo a single person.

And now he wanted something, someone. She was the someone who had appeared. He probably believed he had summoned her. And now she wondered: Had she summoned him? Why? And out of what coffin hidden away in what cellar or attic? She smiled at the image, borrowed from some black and white horror film. What would her grandmother say? The familiar firm voice was suddenly in her head: "He isn't worth the breath of a fly on a mirror. Send him back where he came from."

The magician hugged himself and shivered. "You were at that party, right?"

She looked across the street behind him, at a shabby, turquoise three-storey with an uncharacteristically well-groomed lawn. The moonlight glassed the grass, turning it into a silver crew cut. The magician was quite high, and by the smell of him, so drunk that if she struck a match she would catch his breath on fire. She remembered Marianela, a buzz-headed friend from Calgary who used to read her tarot when she lived there. Marianela was tiny, barely five feet tall and probably ninety pounds, but she wore heavy black boots and frighteningly thick leather belts. She cut hair for a living and drank whisky as a hobby. And she often walked home alone. One night Marianela had been followed by a luggish lumberjack type. "I'm going to rape you!" he bellowed. "You'd better watch out! I'm going to rape you!" This had gone on for blocks, the lumberjack yelling at her back, Marianela growing more and more incensed. Finally, a few blocks from her house, she stopped and turned to face him. She planted her feet squarely and waited. As he barrelled toward her, she lifted one foot and kicked him as hard as she could in the balls. He stumbled to the ground and she ran, terrified and laughing, home.

Where was Marianela now? And what had her grandmother said about getting rid of flies? Where were those scissors she had used to sever bad energetic ties? She recalled her grandmother giggling as she waved burning sage throughout the house, as she tied a bit of mint to the broom. What had that been for? And what about the little horse-headed stick she had given Angela for her seventh birthday? How she had loved that toy, riding it around the neighbourhood like a hero, its yarn mane flying. Would that it was here now, so she could fly away. Yet, she felt the wind on her face and the traces of gin glinting a cold clarity in her blood and she did not feel afraid. She would talk to this stranger, this magician of unfortunate jokes, his white face hanging in front of hers like a forgotten ornament on a January Christmas tree. She would talk to him for just a moment and then she would cross the street, or he would cross the street, slink back to his house, back to the shed or tent or draughty room he slept in.

"Yes, I was at the party," she said. "And you..."

Just as she started to question him, he lurched forward, tottering for a moment, and then abruptly fell back, sitting heavily on the curb.

"I'm gone," he said. His pale face glowed greenish, glossy with cold sweat.

She could see he wasn't acting; he was indeed severely wasted. Yet she could feel no sympathy for him. At any minute he could lunge up and grab her throat. At any minute, also, she could kick him with her boots, now that he was down. His neck glowed whitely vulnerable through the strands of his black hair. She felt her hands burning in her pockets. She was prepared to hit him if that's what it would take. She curled her hands into fists and dug them deeper into her pockets. Something cold and angular poked her. Her phone. She could call someone. But who? Jake's ringer probably wasn't on. And even if she did answer—what then? She would enter the scene as a hero, intent on saving the damsel in distress. Jake wouldn't be able to help it—she would have to punch this pathetic man, who would end up in the exact same position he was in now, except his nose would be broken and he would be bleeding into the street.

Angela had never seen her grandmother hit anyone. Her grandmother wouldn't even slap a ghost, though she might kindly sweep one out of the house. But she had once seen her after an argument whip a rug against the stairs so violently it seemed it might explode into a fury of thread. Her grandmother had been capable of harnessing tremendous rage. And her grandmother had taught her that there were people you should avoid and people you would want to avoid but wouldn't be able to. But what was the trick to get rid of such people?

At her feet, the magician leaned closer toward the street and started retching. A pool of pinkish bile formed at his feet. In between pukes he gasped for breath. "Water," he said weakly.

Angela suddenly felt weary, the weight of the long night heavy upon her. She should be home by now, stirring honey into a mug of strong ginger tea, lighting a candle and running a bath. She loved the smell of just-washed hair, the feel of fresh sheets as she slipped between them. She loved going to sleep alone as the sun was starting to rise, as the rest of the world was waking up.

And now she remembered what to do. She would keep walking. That was the spell: To keep walking. To say a few words if one had to, but to keep walking. She relaxed her hand around her phone. Her grandmother had seldom used the phone when she was living, and Angela didn't need a phone to reach her now.

"Hey," the magician feebly called after her as she started to cross the street. "Hey." And then more weakly, "You bitch." His voice floated down to the concrete like a lost feather.

She felt her shoulders lift as she reached the opposite curb. Her feet felt light in her boots, the sidewalk solid beneath her. A lamp clicked on in one of the dark houses. Angela tightened her coat around her and looked up at the lightening sky.

THE RASH

He was most of all very nice. He collected stuffed tigers—his bed was covered with them. He had a large bed that he had never managed to share with anyone. He had purple curtains his father had sewn for him when he first moved out. His mother had died years before, leaving him no money and a dowry of sadness.

Yet he appeared to be a cheerful man. He wore smart grey suits and orange socks. Purple socks with white polka dots on meeting days. He loved the royalness of purple—wanted a purple velvet couch with purple velvet cushions. He imagined himself slouching seductively on it, pants unbuttoned.

At the bathhouse he was lonely. His paunch, the camping scars on his calves, the inexplicable rash on his face and neck. He still had his thick, black hair, curly, cut short—his only beauty. Other men seldom cruised him. A cloudy dense aura surrounded him that no amount of looking or fucking ever managed to thin.

Sometimes a cock ended up in his mouth or a fist in his ass—

he was always surprised, too surprised to be grateful. Before he could ever speak, it was over. He went home with a heavy feeling in his chest, a desire to shower and sleep for a dozen hours.

Maybe it was his smoking. Not the smoking itself, but the fact that he pretended he didn't. He hid it unsuccessfully from his father and his colleagues and his friends. The musky cologne he favoured tinged the smokiness with an animal scent. He believed he smoked to keep his weight down, although his belly continued to grow. Late at night, working on budgets he should have finished at the office, he lit cigarette after cigarette and gorged on chocolate. He felt sad, jealous, bored, horny, and something else he couldn't name. It was a feeling—not a nice one—alternately an ache or an itch. It made him sick and desperate. He woke to an archipelago of pimples on his chin, the rash itching on his forehead. His doctor prescribed steroid cream. His therapist prescribed calm. His friends prescribed more beers, more beaches.

Saturdays his father would call and ask him about his work, his rash, any potential boyfriends. Hungover, the son pieced together amusing anecdotes, but never told his father about his nights at the bathhouse. They talked about the missing mother, her strong Earl Grey and snappy comebacks, whether roses, daisies or lilies for the grave this Mother's Day and did you hear her friend Betsy died? More cancer.

Before the conversation got too maudlin, his father would always change the subject to a good *Toronto Star* book review or a new pesto chicken recipe. He would email it over. He would make it the next time the son came to visit. The father always ended the conversations with reassurances of love. "I know you will find someone soon," he often said, as if loneliness was his son's only problem.

The man tried to shine a niceness though his fog. But there was always this feeling he could never identify. It hung around his neck like a heavy iron amulet. His therapist had never prescribed magic of any kind. And in their conversations, his father had never mentioned his own singlehood, his own desires. The mother dead twelve years.

Was it her death that had left the son with this feeling? Why he could never feel at home on his imaginary purple couch, at his computer, in the bars with his friends? Why he always shrivelled back into himself after he came, why he often woke up sweating before his alarm went off, curled in a ball as if protecting some fragile part of himself?

He felt like there was a pane of glass between him and the rest of the world. Cellophane clinging to his face. Sometimes, when driving to meet friends at the bar, he felt like he couldn't breathe, that his palpitating heart might burst from its cage. He would pull over and light a cigarette, roll down the window and fan the air in front of his face. Then he would count, blankly count, until his heartbeat slowed.

His mother had smoked nearly her whole life. On breaks at the fish cannery in her late teens. Later as an office girl in pencil skirts and heels. And finally on her deathbed, hooked up to an oxygen machine. His father had never complained. Had never spoken of it. Just opened the windows of the house and sprayed chemical-smelling air fresheners in the living room. Just bought his wife cartons and, at her request, left packs throughout the house—on the back of the toilet, in the kitchen cupboard next to the plates. His mother would often interrupt her stirring of tomato sauce or chopping of potatoes to light a cigarette, gesticulating to make a point with the fiery tip as his father nodded in agreement. His father was a smiler, a peacemaker and a back-patter. It was from him that the son learned to lie, to keep quiet or change the subject when asked direct questions. His father smiled and nodded for years, right up until the lithium stopped working and his hospitalized wife screamed in pain and rage. Then his father sat down on the chair next to her bed, cradled his face in his hands, and finally sobbed.

In the dim green halls of the hospital, after it was over, the two men held each other as nurses and doctors and orderlies streamed by. "We are alone now," his father had said. "We are each other's only family now."

Months later, over a waffle brunch cooked by the father, each admitted that, during those last painful days, he had thought of taking the pillow from under the mother's head and carefully, firmly, placing it over her face. This was the only act of compassion left to them, and neither had been able to do it.

The man was sick of his cowardice and sick of his rash and sick to death of his loneliness. At a patio party he refused the proffered joint and a friend asked him, "What are you so afraid of?" The question stayed with him for days. He knew the answer but couldn't bring himself to articulate it.

He was afraid of everything.

When he was in third grade he had brought his friend James home from school. In his room, the play turned to touching, to taking off shirts and pants. James's skin was smooth, soft and golden. He had a laugh like a bright little bell. As the two boys were stroking each other, the door opened—his mother. She didn't look surprised or angry. She simply told the two boys to put on their clothes and come to the kitchen for a snack. She had baked oatmeal cookies.

Later in the afternoon, after James left, his mother had sat him down on the couch. Lighting a cigarette, she blew the smoke out the window and told him that what he and James had done was natural and nothing to be ashamed of.

"Children are curious," he remembered her saying. "They explore. It's their nature."

Yet he had felt a deep burning sensation and a wish to disappear into the green, linty cushions of the couch, to hide under the floral rug. He didn't want her to know about his private feelings. He didn't want her to see him.

His mother didn't say anything else, just finished her cigarette and then patted his knee before getting up to make dinner.

Years later, when he had come out in his early twenties, she had brought up this incident.

"That boy James? Your sweet friend?"

He had coldly denied the memory, had told her he didn't know what she was talking about and asked angrily why she was saying this, when he was trying to share with her, trying to tell her something that was very difficult to tell, that he had been keeping inside for some time.

His mother had not apologized. She had not denied his story either. She had simply asked him if he was happy now, if he felt more free. And although it was a relief to tell her, there was still a churning in his gut, a horrible feeling that was not relief, was not freedom. Where had the feeling come from? And when? He could not remember ever having lived without it. He remembered lying in bed as a child, young, three, four years old, feeling like there was something wrong with him, that he had done something wrong, but he didn't know what.

"Yes," he had lied. "I'm happy. I'm finally happy now."

And his mother had said she was glad, glad to hear it, but he could tell from her tone that she knew he was lying. Soon after, they both hung up, and he went out to the bars to celebrate finally telling her, although at the same time, he wondered why he had waited so long. Compared to his many friends who had been yelled at, cried over, pleaded with, hit, kicked, thrown out, and disowned, his coming out was a nothing, not even a blip on the line of his life. His parents had never taught him that there was anything wrong with being gay. This could not be, he realized then, the source of the feeling.

One morning he woke from a drenched, drunk sleep with a word in his head. *Unworthy*. He held the word between his teeth. It soured his mouth like a sip of old beer. Finally he released it into the stale air of his dark bedroom: *Unworthy*. His rash burned. He was afraid to get up and look in the mirror, afraid it might have spread down his neck, to his chest. He stumbled to the window to pull open the purple curtains.

Rainy cold light seeped into the room. It was already winter again. He felt panic like sharp little pins in his chest. There was nothing to be scared of, nothing to be sad about, he told himself. He thought of calling someone, a friend, his father. But he knew he had nothing nice to say. And when he didn't have anything nice to say, he didn't say anything. He didn't say anything at all.

INSOMNIA

Insomnia. She was born one day out of the shadows of my closet. She lived there for months, and then she moved in with me.

She started working at the cafe where I took my coffee each morning. She wore bright blue nail polish and black lipstick and, licking her lips, told every customer she was pregnant. She ignored me and only served my coffee when it was cold. After her shift, she would follow me home and collapse in my bed, snoring, her red hair billowing like theatre curtains. I started to sleep on the couch.

One morning I woke up to her giving me a tattoo on my foot with a sharpened chopstick and ink from a discarded ink cartridge she'd found in my garbage. The tattoo was a startling likeness of her face. She worked diligently until it was done.

Her stomach grew. It was a hysterical pregnancy, but very convincing—to her, and to everyone else. She told everyone at the cafe the baby was mine. They always looked surprised, but then quickly covered it up. They didn't understand my gender and had no idea what my genitals were capable of.

"I'm down to one coffee a day. My brain just isn't working the same way," she told a regular, an opera singer in a green muumuu. She licked her lips. "Green, my favourite colour. Money and jealousy..." But the woman turned away in disgust.

Insomnia's flirting skills were abominable—even I couldn't be seduced by her, though she slept in my bed every night.

Nine months passed and Insomnia's stomach kept getting bigger. She stole sheets from my bed to sew herself an elaborate pregnancy dress that looked like a bridal gown, complete with a train. She started telling customers at the cafe that we were getting married.

At this time, she would only eat sushi from one particular neighbourhood shop and had given up coffee completely. Her stomach grew and grew. She started calling herself "the mansion": "No mere *house* could hold *her.*" Her—she had also decided her baby was a girl, claiming the ultrasound showed a certain body part particular to that category of human.

Insomnia's ideas of what a girl was were very strange. Girls were terrors and beauties. Girls should shave their heads at eighteen. Girls often killed small creatures and painted their faces and arms with blood. Girls shouldn't be given coffee before the age of twenty-one. Girls were builders, first and foremost. Girls should never have babies.

She bought a huge, pink stuffed elephant and slept with it in my bed. Afternoons after work, she would flop on the couch, leaving the elephant to doze in my room. I had nowhere to sleep. She ignored me, cooked elaborate meals—meaty pastas, nutty salads, fragrant orange curries—and ate them all at my kitchen table while I rested, hungry, on a camping mat on the kitchen floor.

The customers and neighbours started to become suspicious. It had been a year since she first announced she was pregnant. Her stomach was still growing. "*Three* months late?" they'd ask. "Have you seen a doctor?"

She would airily brush aside their concerns, "You know how doctors are. Another latte?"

Soon the cafe owner wanted to fire her. Her freakishness was bad for business. Her outfits, sewn from my curtains, tablecloths, and pillowcases, became more and more outrageous. Deep cleavage, eye-holes to show her belly button, skirts tight on her thighs and slit up the leg. Her flirting had gotten even more aggressive, her makeup more garish. She smelled like cottage cheese and old rosewater. Everyone was either bored of her or scared of her.

After being fired, Insomnia came back to my apartment, back to my bed, and slept. She slept all day, and she slept all night. For many days, and for many nights. At first, I tried to comfort her. I brought her chamomile tea and apples, a little bit of chocolate to brighten her face. But she would just turn her head away. After a week, I let her be, hoping she would rouse herself without my interference. But several more days passed in unbearable silence, the bedroom door resolutely closed. When I put my ear to the door, I couldn't hear any movement.

Finally, I knocked softly, and, when there was no reply, I crept into the room. There she was: Insomnia. Naked on her back, the covers thrown aside. I could tell immediately that she had not moved in some time. I stepped closer. Her eyelids were smeared with ancient mascara. Her stomach had deflated like an old balloon, and flopped sadly to one side. Her strong odour had diminished, leaving just a trace of milk and roses. Even her velvety red hair had dulled. I didn't have to hold a mirror in front of her mouth to see that she was not breathing. In death she looked shrunken and green.

Outside the window, dark clouds raced, and as I watched, the shadows gathering in the room started to slide across her face and arms. Her birth shadows, come to take her home again. I bent over and picked her up.

The afternoon was darkening rapidly as I climbed into the closet with Insomnia in my arms.

THIRD BEACH

They were ex-wives. Of each other. It was summer. Just past spring. Time for flings. Picnics, vodka lemonade, croquet. Swimming in deep and shallow waters.

One ex-wife was looking sexy in a retro green bikini with a built-in, cone-shaped bra. She seemed taller than she had the summer before, her legs longer, her toenails redder. The other ex-wife had been going to the gym since the break-up. Her blue one-piece showed off her strong hairy calves, her sculpted arms. Highlights glinted in her frizzy brown hair and her black-framed glasses made her look as serious as ever, although she laughed and laughed, sprinting across the sand, grabbing a friend's ass, diving for the Frisbee.

It was another potluck-birthday-going-away party. Herons fished at the water's edge, seagulls dove lazily above them. Five, ten, then twenty people sipped warm ciders, smoked joints so fat they stretched the papers they were rolled in. Blankets and towels spread with crackers and olives, goat cheese and fruit, chocolate and nuts. Gossiping and swimming as the afternoon swung into evening and the sand started to chill under their feet. Then it was sparkling wine from a friend's backpack, a driftwood bonfire, candles wedged in the sand, and dancing to the tinny, tiny music from someone's phone.

The sexy one came back from peeing in the woods, flushed and laughing. She had stumbled upon a stand-off between a skunk and a raccoon, but the skunk had finally slunk away without spraying her. She fanned out her armpits with her hands as if releasing the smell that could have been. Her stories were always like that, tumbling and flawless.

Standing so close, the serious one could smell the salt of seawater, the warmth of sun on her. She had heard that she had dumped her boyfriend the week before. When she put her arm around the sexy one's shoulders, she could feel the flat wet blanket of her blond hair, still dripping from her swim.

Of course, the sexy one was the first to take her shirt off when the moon rose, to yell "Skinny dip!" and then race to the water. The serious one had not seen her breasts in eighteen months. In the flickering firelight, her nipples were mysterious, desirable. She took a chug of cider and could only think of them in her mouth.

A week later they ran into each other on a street lined with bookstores, boutiques, and coffee shops in the neighbourhood where they used to live, where the serious one still lived. Neither had anywhere to be that day. At the corner cafe, they ordered espressos and shared a chocolate chip cookie. The sun was hot through the windows, the coffee very strong, the barista flirtatious and significantly tattooed. The sexy one wore pink lipstick and a new vanilla scent, her grey eyes bright between mascaraed lashes. She called her ex-boyfriend self-centred and mopey and told funny stories about their relationship. The serious one laughed at everything she said.

It was only a few short blocks to the serious one's apartment.

After a year, more than a year, after a year and six months, her kisses were deep water, her skin the softest apricot. The sweetest vinegar between her legs. She had gotten even better at spanking. Her sweat had taken on a different tone, milkish, slightly sour, as if she was sweating out the scent of her most recent lover.

That night in bed, the serious one sat up and read a poem. Not an entire poem, but an excerpt from a very long, very famous poem by someone dead. Parts of the poem were still quite good. She chose a few lines about happiness being all around us, how we can pluck it out of the air just by breathing. Then she lay back down. It was true, she thought. Happiness could be that easy. Like breathing. And she turned to the sexy one and started kissing her again.

They did their best to keep it a secret from their friends. But within days they were seen holding hands on a certain gay street and later at the grocery store picking out a watermelon and after that it was common knowledge.

A mutual friend called the serious one. "You two are so perfect for each other it's sickening. I don't know why you ever broke up."

"We're just hanging out," said the serious one.

"But you're back together."

"Not really."

"You're dating."

"I wouldn't call it that."

"What would you call it?"

"Hanging out. Like I said. We're hanging out."

This friend hadn't been satisfied with her answer, and other friends had called and texted, but the serious one never changed her story. It was just a summer fling. They weren't getting back together. It was fun. It was summer. It was just a light summer thing.

For weeks they fisted and kissed and fucked and stroked and slapped each other. As they crossed railroad tracks on the way to omelette breakfasts, as they biked to each other's apartments after work, as they slept and sweated and dreamt, as they went to the movies or met for cocktails—each secretly hoped that the other would change her mind.

They had married seven years earlier, in June. It had been a beach wedding, a sunny day with seagulls and a few clouds, their friends in white pants and lavender dresses, pink suits and shorts, bikinis and rainbow boas. Encircling them were jars of foxgloves picked from a friend's garden. The white-haired marriage commissioner stood by as they read the words they had so carefully written for one another.

"I will love you until my heart kicks out," the serious one had said.

"I honour your freedom, beautiful creature," the sexy one vowed through tears.

"May happiness be your companion and your days together be good and long upon the earth," the lesbian marriage commissioner solemnly said. Then she smiled widely. "It is my great pleasure now to pronounce you married. You may now kiss and dance wildly."

And their friends cheered and cried and jumped up and down on the sand. One friend started up on his bongo drums as another sawed away at her cello. Everyone shimmied and pranced to the music, the champagne corks popping like fireworks.

The serious one remembers this day as she spoons her ex-wife, smelling the musky, vanilla sweat at the back of her neck. It's a humid August day and they've been fucking since mid-morning. Hot sun bakes the red curtains and fills the room with pink light. She wants to say something about that day but she doesn't dare. Saying something would mean it, this thing they are doing, is serious. And it's not serious, although it's been seven weeks and at times, when they are about to fall asleep together, or when they are on the phone about to say goodbye, it seems like there is more to say, like something is going to break through the surface of the conversation. But then they just fall asleep or hang up, and she always feels lonely until she sees the sexy one again and can kiss her face.

Their bodies are so familiar to each other. The scar on the ridge of the elbow from the motorcycle accident, the crooked nose from the missed catch while playing softball. The hairs crawling from the crotch down to the leg, the hairs crawling up to meet the belly button. The mole on the left breast, the soft flesh of the inner thigh, the strangely small second toe, the paths carved by stretch marks. They hold each other as they've held each other thousands of times, slick with sweat in the hot box of her bedroom.

How did it end? The serious one has a hard time remembering. Her memories of that time are scenes seen through a rainy windshield periodically scraped by wipers. She can sometimes catch a glimpse—a clear image, a crystallized thought—but mostly it is a blurry wet painting of dark January days, cold notes left on tables, nights spent alone, nausea, insomnia, crying phone calls to friends, and finally hopelessness, boxes packed and papers signed.

But how did it end?

They fell out of love.

No, that's not quite it.

They never fell out of love.

The sexy one fell out of lust and fell into bed with someone else. The serious one fell out of trust.

What a bad poem of a break-up it was.

But how did it end?

The sexy one fell out of lust and...

No, that's not quite it.

There was this other thing, this thing they never really talked about until the last months of their relationship. This thing, early on, they thought they had agreed upon—a discussion had once and never revisited. This thing they still have a hard time talking about.

The sexy one has always been more brave. And so it is she who says, after seven and a half weeks, "I think we should talk. About this. I mean, us. What we're doing." They are on the phone, planning their next date. "Let's meet at the beach. I'll bring some paper and we can draw."

By *draw*, the serious one knows she means *map*. The sexy one loves maps, any maps, she used to cover their apartment walls with them, buy antique globes from thrift stores and stuff them into tall bookshelves. The serious one always wondered why she was so obsessed with everywhere that wasn't where they were.

At the beach, it is windy. The sun is out, but fall lurks in a slight chill. The serious one has brought green tea in a thermos and a basket of blueberries. When she arrives, the sexy one is already there, unrolling a big piece of brown butcher paper and attempting to secure the corners with large rocks. As the serious one approaches, she sees there are already words and pictures drawn on the paper.

"So you got a head start, I see," she says, setting down her backpack.

"I thought it would be a good idea. To map out a few things before we met." The sexy one has pulled her hair back in a scarf, but a few escaped strands whip her face.

"But we won't be able to draw on the sand."

"I'm just laying it out to show you. We can put it on this"—
she pulls a large art book out of her bag—"when we want to add
to it."

They kiss and the serious one keeps one hand on the small of
her back, the other gripping her upper arm. The sexy one doesn't
say anything, but the serious one can feel that she wants her to
let go, and so, finally, she does.

They sit on either side of the map and eat blueberries and
some bread the sexy one baked. They stare at the map. The serious one sees what looks like a bridge and some rose bushes.
She sees the word "promise" and the word "fun."

"I want to add something," she says, her mouth full of bread.

"What?"

"I want to draw something. On the map."

"Okay." The sexy one rifles around in her bag for a pen and
gives it to her.

The serious one pulls the art book onto her lap and part of
the map on top of it.

"What are these bushes for?"

The sexy one raises an eyebrow and laughs. "Guess."

"Seriously though."

"They're us. Duh."

"Not just our bushes," the serious one attempts to joke.

"See how there's a bridge between them?"

"But what's that under the bridge? A boat? I really wish you'd
waited for me to do this." The serious one sips her tea and puts
a blueberry in her mouth.

"You can add to it now. Go ahead."

Next to the word "fun," the serious one writes, "Is it?" On the bridge, she draws two stick figures. She pauses. And then draws a third, with a stick penis. She glares at the sexy one.

"Hey! Play nice. What's he doing on the bridge? He has nothing to do with us." The sexy one tucks a strand of hair into her scarf.

"He's the reason we broke up."

"He is *not*. *We* are the reason we broke up. We are. But this map isn't about that. That's the past. It's about us now. Where we're going from here. What we're doing."

"I don't want to do it." The serious one lays the pen down on the sand and holds her teacup with both hands, looking out at the water. "I don't want to make a map."

"Honey, we have to."

"No, we don't."

"Then what are we going to do?"

"We're going to sit here and enjoy the beach." A seagull screeches overhead and splatters a wet pile of shit on the log beside her. They both look at it and laugh, then look tentatively at each other.

A chilly wind stirs up the beach, but that doesn't stop the sexy one from getting up and pulling off her dress. She is wearing the same retro bikini she wore at the beach party two months ago. She spreads out her arms and smiles, then turns and runs into the waves.

The serious one holds the map against her lap and wants to let go of it, to let it blow away. But she knows she can't. The map is not a record of where they are going. It is a record of where they have been. She flattens it with her palm and reaches for the pen. She will draw it then. The thing between them. The thing they haven't been able to talk about. She will draw it. She starts with a crescent shape, a new moon. Then another one. She adds little curved spikes. Eyelashes. Then small circles for nostrils, a little bowtie of a mouth. The peaceful face of a sleeping baby. The baby one of them wants and one of them doesn't.

She looks up and sees her ex-wife splashing in the waves, kicking up her feet and laughing like a child. The sun is starting to sink behind her, lighting up the sails on the boats and making the freighters glimmer.

The wind picks up again, whipping the waves. She takes a sip of her tea but it's already cold. She has no sweater, so she wraps her arms around herself.

THE SISTERS AND THE ASH

When the mother slipped to ghost, the three sisters were left with her rings and her teapot and her hairbrushes full of long grey hair. They were left with a grey house, stained walls, and a very drunk father, his belt and his rage.

The mother had not known how to protect them. And then she became too weak to leave her bed. But the sisters were smart, each one smarter than the last, and they learned how to protect themselves.

While on a camping trip in the mountains, the eldest met an old but agile crone who lived in a cave. From the crone, she learned an obscure martial art that she quickly mastered and taught to her sisters. Each sister slept with a beautifully jewelled knife—a surprising parting gift from the mother—tucked under her pillow.

One night, the father came into the youngest sister's room to massage her feet. She struck him so hard in the chest that he fell backward. From the floor he saw her knife glittering above him like a menacing star.

After that, the father began to live in earnest fear. He took up the anxious habits of one afraid. Smoking. Pacing. His old addictions—yelling, beating, and drinking—were no longer allowed. He dared not smoke in the house after his middle daughter's strident lecture on second-hand cancer. He cowered in the corners of the rooms, covering his words with coughs. The sisters pretended he wasn't there—and indeed, he became nearly invisible to them, just a light mildew dusting the baseboards, fading to green-grey mist.

One day, the eldest sister entered the living room carrying a soapy sponge and a bucket and the father retreated to the garage to hide among the rusty car parts and old sports magazines. Chain-smoking, he'd leaf through swimsuit issues, looking at breasts and thighs, the hint of a carefully shaved mound. But even the youngest bodies were like dead wood to him. Nothing plucked his imagination. A lead-stomached grief filled him, where once had been virile rage.

In his absence, the house became cheery. The sisters washed all the walls and painted them bright cherry, sassy turquoise, I-caught-a-canary yellow. The father's ratty furniture and smelly clothes made a heavenly bonfire when burned with sticks of fragrant incense. There were late and loud parties, stomping dances, music of horn and saxophone and trumpet, each sister emptying her lungs into song. It was as if their father had never been born, had never lived.

Years passed. The sisters took lovers and let them go, deepened friendships, learned trades, grew an abundant garden. The middle sister became a brother. The youngest had a child they collectively raised. They had long forgotten the father when one day the youngest sister went out to mow the lawn and noticed a ghost ship—the garage—sagging at the edge of their property. She thought it would make a nice art studio for the child.

The door was bolted from inside. She had to kick it open. Dust upon dust—she could barely see for all the motes stirred up in the air. At the back of the garage, she saw a shrunken figure balanced between a bench and a worktable. She stepped closer. Under a thick layer of dust was a skeleton barely held together by the thin paper of its dried skin. Between two fingers, a cigarette, a long fingernail of ash at its tip.

The daughter blew softly and watched as her father crumbled to dust.

THE FOX

She called her black dick Licorice, her red dick Satan, and her sparkly dick The Unicorn.

She rode a motorcycle, of course, but I never got to ride on it.

She was supposed to take me for a spin on our first date, but she showed up with her arm in a sling and a big scratch on her face.

"Catfight?" I joked.

She grimaced. "Accident." We started to walk to the restaurant. On the way, we talked about meditation. She had just returned from a ten-day retreat.

"I hated him," she said, referring to the teacher. "His voice just droned on, drove me fucking crazy. So full of himself. As if he already knew everything." She snorted.

"Maybe he——" I ventured.

"It was boring, anyway," she interrupted. "Meditation is boring and painful. My knees hurt so bad." With that, she took my elbow and steered me into the restaurant.

Even though one of her arms was immobilized, Willis han-
dled me with the same confidence she had on the night we had
met. I had been drunk, sitting alone while my date's band dirged
onstage. Willis sauntered up, set a pint of beer in front of me and
sat down at my table. "Hi," she had said, as if the word held some
special meaning known only to the two of us. I mumbled something about the volume of the music and being less than sober.
We watched the bands without speaking for a few moments, and
then she started a conversation about past lives and how I looked
familiar, how she had noticed me the moment she walked into
the bar. I wondered: had she noticed me making out with my date
all over the room? She turned to me intently, holding my blue
eyes with her green ones. "I want to get to know you better," she
said, reaching for my hand across the table. "There's just something about you. Something..." She grasped my hand as if we
were already intimates.

I laughed and took a chug of my beer. She had no idea who I
was. We had barely spoken. Yet there was something charming
about her presumptuousness. I knew I was supposed to be flat-
tered by her attention, and I allowed myself to be.

Usually I was the one who made the moves. It had taken me
weeks of courtship to finally get into the briefs of my current
date, who drummed away onstage behind a tangle of black hair
with a passion that belied her trademark shyness. I normally
went for the quiet girls, the awkward ones in boy's clothes with
ball caps tilted down low to hide their hungry eyes. But Willis
had something. Her thick red hair was cut short, speckled with
grey and white like the coat of a fox. Her eyes were bright with

sobriety and desire. She emitted a certain energy, a certain magnetism. When she held my hand and traced the lines in my palm with one of her fingers, I felt a pulse between my legs.

Her eyes darted over my shoulder at someone in the shadows near the back of the bar. She set my hand back down on the table.

"I'll be right back," she said. "Stay here."

She disappeared into the crowd. In front of me, people swayed to the music, blocking my view of the stage. The band played mournfully, as if they knew all our troubles and wanted to release them for us through their songs. I closed my eyes and let the music fill me.

After a few minutes Willis returned and sat back down, picking up my hand and holding it with both of hers. "I couldn't find her," she said. "Weird. She was cruising me all night and I finally went to talk to her and she disappeared." She smiled and looked meaningfully into my eyes again. "Where were we?"

Despite this jarring beginning, I had given her my phone number, had kissed her in the dark hallway by the bathroom while my date's band was packing up their gear. And now I was sitting across from her at a vegetarian Mexican joint owned by white hipsters who did all the deliveries by bicycle. The place buzzed with conversation and laughter. Retro bicycles hung from the walls and ferns hung in jars from the ceiling.

I had found out from our phone conversation the night before that she was a vegan and a health nut. This had surprised me. I had never met a vegan who rode a motorcycle. The two things seemed at odds, though I couldn't say why. Perhaps I was under the influence of stereotypes—my mind clutched by images of bikers, dusty and leather-clad, wolfing down hamburgers and thick milkshakes at roadside diners.

She perused the menu while attempting to play footsie with me under the table. I wore my new checkered sneakers for the date, and a white button-up men's shirt purchased at Goodwill. She had told me on the walk to the restaurant that that was one of the things that had drawn her to me: my style.

"I'm getting so bored of girly girls," she had said. "I like that you're a tomboy. Tomboys are sexy."

The label of "tomboy" irked me, but I hadn't said anything. Instead I picked up the menu and turned the pages, avoiding her eyes.

She stopped running her boot up my calf and reached across the table for my hand. I had to set down the menu to grab back. "What are you getting?" she asked.

"I don't know," I said. "I didn't get much of a chance to look at the menu."

"Oh, right, sorry." She blushed slightly as she retracted her hand. I picked up the menu again.

"Who was that girl at the club the other night?" she asked.

"Who?"

"The one in the band."

"Darcy?"

"I don't know her name. The Chinese one."

I set the menu down and took a sip of my water. "She's not Chinese. She's Vietnamese. Her name is Darcy."

"Does she know you're out with me right now?"

"Of course."

"So you're open."

"Yes."

She eyed me suspiciously. "You're not one of those poly people, are you? Because I'm not really into that. Are you in some poly group?"

The mohawked server appeared and set an iced tea in front of her and a pale ale in front of me, smirking as she sauntered away. Willis looked down at her menu, then up at me, slightly embarrassed that her question had been overheard. Then her face shifted back to its usual expression, confidence underlain with something I couldn't quite identify. She raked her straw back and forth through her tea.

"No, I'm not in a group." I took a sip of my beer. "I'm not really that poly. I'm just dating Darcy right now."

"And me, I hope." She winked. "We're on a date, right?"

I was surprised by a sudden wave of shyness that turned my face red. I picked at the damp label on my beer and tried to think of something to say. "So, do you meditate daily, or what?"

"Oh no," she said dismissively. "I haven't meditated since I got back."

"Which was?"

"Two months ago. I lost a lot of weight, though. At the retreat." She smiled broadly. "I had to buy new jeans."

I wasn't sure what to say to this. She was thin and athletic, had told me she lifted weights at the gym and ran three times a week. I took another sip of my beer. "Um, you had to fast?"

"Oh no, you eat. Just not very much and not very often. Only two meals, early in the day. You get so hungry. And that made me angry at first."

"Hangry," I joked.

"Yeah," she laughed. "Hangry. I was really hangry at first, especially after the evening tea, when your stomach is growling and it's only six o'clock and you're like, fuck, when am I going to eat again."

"It sounds rough," I offered.

"It wasn't so bad." She pushed her iced tea to the side of the table and reached for my hands again, to indicate the conversation was finished.

Later that night, we fucked for the first time. The foreplay was long and tortuous; it involved her showing me two episodes of her favourite reality show about starving bitchy models and their managers, and making me look through a photo album full of pictures from her childhood: Little Willis wearing cowboy shirts, sitting on horses; Willis eating ice cream with her aunts; toddler Willis in a little blue swimsuit; Willis with bedhead and chocolate smeared on her face. Halfway through the album, my libido was almost nonexistent and my beer buzz from the restaurant was gone. "Can we look at the rest of these another time?" I asked. "I mean, it's a little overwhelming right now. I'm a little overwhelmed."

"Oh. I'm sorry." Her apology had a slight air of affront. She quickly took the album from my lap and put it back on her bookshelf. We were sitting on her couch and her computer was still streaming bad TV, but the sound was off. She wrapped her good arm around me and nuzzled my neck. I was still feeling put off, but when she stuck her tongue in my ear and starting slowly rubbing my nipples with her thumb, I became aroused in spite of myself.

"Let's go upstairs," she whispered. "I want to show you some things."

Her bedroom was dominated by a king-sized bed covered with a red velvet duvet and black pillows. She lit a few candles while I examined the pictures on her walls. She had a shrine set up under one of her windows, with a small goddess statue in the centre, a string of prayer beads at her feet.

"I thought you didn't meditate," I said to her, as she placed a candle on the bedside table.

"I don't," she said.

"Then why do you have this altar?"

"Nostalgia." She laughed. "My ex was a witch. Sort of. She got me into all that stuff. So everywhere I move, I make an altar. It's just part of my routine now."

I nodded. I also had a shrine at my place, but I wasn't going to tell her that. At least not yet. I didn't know if she'd ever see my place. I tried to feel the desire that had pulsed just moments before, but I couldn't locate it.

She set down the final candle and suddenly lunged for me, pushing me to the bed with her good arm and slowly lowering herself down next to me. I felt the full length of her body against mine, her hip bones, her breasts, and I again felt turned on. Her tongue moved insistently in my mouth, trying to tell me something. I kissed her back while a part of me wondered if I really wanted to have sex with her. I turned my mind away from this question and started to unbutton her shirt.

Her breasts were flat, all nipple, and the nipples weren't very responsive. She seemed embarrassed by this. "I don't know why I don't get them pierced," she said, as I bit and tugged at them. "That would give them more sensation." She bent down to bite at my neck. "You're so dreamy."

This came off as yet another line. Several times over the course of the evening, I had the distinct impression that what she was saying to me she had said many times before. Her compliments sounded especially rehearsed. "I like your tough walk," she had whispered to me as we exited the restaurant. I didn't know what she was talking about. My walk had a feminine bounce that was lovingly parodied by my friends. When I first came out, I had tried to learn how to swagger, but it didn't become me, so I abandoned it. My walk was just mine, I had finally concluded. It was good enough. But it was a far cry from tough.

She sat up, straddling me, and with slow, careful effort, unbuttoned my shirt with her good hand. Then she pulled up my undershirt and sports bra, fondling my breasts sentimentally. "These are beautiful," she said, cupping one in her hand. "I'm going to call this one Bella." She moved her hand to the other breast, holding it with a studied tenderness. "And this one. This one... I don't have a name for yet." She smiled with that strange, super-

ficial confidence of hers. It was clear to me that this wasn't the first
time she had named a lover's breast Bella. I wondered if she had
been about to give my other breast another name she had given
to an ex-lover's breast, and at the last minute had thought better
of it. Maybe, out of respect for our connection, she had decided
to give at least one of my breasts its own unique name, one she
hadn't used before. Or perhaps she had called *both* of her ex-
lover's breasts Bella, and in the moment she couldn't think of any
other name for my second breast.

She rolled off of me and awkwardly sat up on the bed. She
crouched down on the floor, and, with difficulty, pulled a large
shoebox out from under her bed using her free hand. She lifted
it onto the velvet blanket and flipped open the lid. Inside were
several silicon cocks and a leather harness. She pulled the cocks
out one by one and laid them on the bed next to each other. As
she laid each one down, she stroked the length of it with her
hand, as if trying to arouse the inert material. She left the harness in the box.

"Here they are," she said, with false nonchalance, looking
shiftily in my direction.

"Quite the assortment you have there." I tried to match her
nonchalance with my own.

She lay back on the bed with her good arm behind her head,
letting the sling lay across her chest. "So, which one do you want
to fuck me with?" she asked.

I was surprised. Usually when a woman pulls out her cock, or
cocks, it means she's going to fuck you. Maybe you'll fuck her
later, but usually, she'll fuck you first. At least, that had been my

experience. And all of her sweet-talking on the walk home had been bent in that direction.

I looked at the array of cocks. I wondered why she bothered to have so many when they were essentially the same size. Of course they had names—she had already whispered their names to me on the walk home from the restaurant, when she put her arm around my waist and slid her hand under my shirt to stroke my back.

I looked at her face to gauge her intention. There was a slight flush to her cheeks and her eyes held desire but were also some-how blank, as if we had already had sex and she was lying alone in her bed a day later remembering it.

But as I looked into her eyes, her gaze deepened into a dare. She was daring me to go for it—to take up my role. To meet her boldness with my own. And although I knew it was just a game, a staged scene, I felt a warmth growing in the pit of my stomach and my breath quickened.

I picked up the red one and felt the weight of it in my palm. I liked its colour and I liked how it felt. "This one," I said. "I'm going to fuck you with this one."

A little bruised and still wet, I let myself out of her apartment early the next morning. It had been raining and the streets shone in the early light. My underwear was crammed into my front pocket and I desperately needed a coffee. There was a coffee shop a few blocks away that I knew would be open. As I turned the corner, my phone buzzed in my back pocket. I pulled it out. Darcy. She couldn't see me tonight, unfortunately. Last minute band practice. Her message came with a supposed-to-be-cute guilty-face emoji. It was the third time in two weeks she had blown me off. I felt tears prick behind my eyes but blinked them away. I knew I was just tired, overreacting. I get that way when I don't have enough sleep.

At the coffee shop I ordered a double espresso and sat at the window so I could watch people walk by. The rain had returned, sloshing down heavily. It seemed like everyone on Main Street had a nice umbrella—bright yellow, zebra print, a pink cityscape against a lightning-streaked sky. Of course I had forgotten mine at home. I pulled out my phone and texted Willis a dirty message, suggesting we meet later in the week. She replied almost instantly, using a cock emoji I'd never seen. "Promises, promises," I texted back. I paused a moment, looking out at the rain, and then included a tongue-lolling-to-the-side smiley face.

We had been hanging out for about a month and Willis's motorcycle was still in the shop. Her arm was no longer in a sling, though, so she picked me up at my house in her roommate's car. She was wearing a new pair of black pants, neatly ironed, and a man's vest with a silver bowtie. A large bulge lifted the zipper of her pants.

"I've got a surprise for you," she said. "Get in."

I was immediately excited by the sight of her. I slid in next to her and put my hand on her thigh.

"I thought I told you to wear a dress. I wanted to put my hands up it," she said.

I knew this was supposed to be a joke, but it still pissed me off.

Whenever a date tried to tell me what to wear, even in jest, I bristled. I had a high school boyfriend who always bought me skimpy clothes and gave me fashion advice. He had loved outrageous colours and had better style than I did. Years later I ran into him at a queer club with his boyfriend. He hugged me and asked kindly about my life, my family, and it was strangely good to see him after all that time, but in high school he was a controlling asshole who wanted me to wear turquoise polka-dot dresses and red heels, tight shiny pants and gold tube tops with high boots. I felt I couldn't say no to the clothes but I hated them and I hated him for making me wear them.

"So, where are we going?" I asked her, removing my hand from her leg.

"I told you," she said. "It's a surprise." She drove silently, her eyes steady on the road. Every once in a while she would reach over and rub my thigh.

She had never come to my house already packing like this. The shape of the bulge suggested a dildo, not just a rolled up sock. I imagined her driving to some deserted road and parking the car under the shade of a tree, slowly unzipping her pants as she looked at me. I envisioned us in the woods, fucking against a tree. But that would make her pants and vest dirty, and she was meticulous about her clothing.

I stared out the window at the shabby apartment buildings and houses with junk piled up on the porches. It was a chilly spring day, clouds and bright shafts of sunlight. A few people were out digging up their gardens. The sight of them made me sad for some reason. I looked over at Willis.

She looked back at me and smiled. "I like your jeans," she said.

This had to be the most generic compliment she had yet to bestow upon me. It was worse even than her rehearsed ones—although they were at times inaccurate, at least they carried a whiff of stale charisma. I felt a surge of annoyance. The jeans were just a regular pair of blue jeans that I had worn on many of our dates. I was sickened that she still had so little of substance to say to me after we had spent so many nights together. I thought of saying something, but stopped myself. What was the point? It would just lead to a fight, and then we wouldn't get to have sex.

Two nights earlier, she had put me in handcuffs and made me scream. I came, I think, about five times, and at one point I had even thought "I love you," but the thought disappeared after I climaxed. Lying in bed afterwards, my hand resting on her sweaty chest, I noticed a spiritual teacher's book on her bedside table. I tried to talk to her about it but she brushed me off, said the book was on loan from a friend and she was just thumbing through it. "It's not very good," she said. "It doesn't really tell me anything I don't already know. I mean, just being on the path you learn a lot."

"What do you mean by 'the path'?" I asked.

"Oh, you know. What we're on. You and me and the other people like us. It's how we're getting closer to our nature."

She often said pseudo-wise things like this, but when I asked questions, she couldn't explain what she meant. She spoke obliquely about herself as someone who had experienced profound spiritual truths, but it was never clear what these truths were. She described a midnight stare-down with a huge owl on a quiet side street, the time a monk on a bus read her mind…it all ended up sounding contrived. A tone of superiority pervaded these stories, and it made me want to disagree with her, to undercut her in some way. But for weeks I had avoided saying anything because I kept thinking each date was going to be our last.

She drove over the bridge and took an exit that let us off in the heart of a little village that had become a popular suburb. It retained some of its quaintness in the form of small, brightly painted cottages with flowerboxes and specialty shops owned by old Germans. She pulled up in front of a pie shop in a small yellow-and-white house. Pies and cupcakes were piled high in the windows on silver platters.

"Here we are," she said, and clamoured out to open the door for me. I noticed she was carrying a black jacket, which she held in front of her as she led me towards the front door.

We got slices of strawberry-rhubarb pie in take-out containers and walked the few blocks to the beach. Willis's gait was a bit stilted, and she kept her jacket in front of her as she walked. I was still mildly titillated. Was she going to fuck me in broad daylight as we rolled around on the sand, or drag me into the cold water to suck her off? I had a hard time imagining that she intended either of these scenarios, for, although performative, she was not an exhibitionist.

The beach was mostly empty, just a few old dog-walkers and one jogger wearing bright pink spandex and headphones. Willis made for a bleached-out log and sat down on it, setting her jacket to the side. Her cock strained against her pants, but she ignored it. I decided I'd better play along and ignore it as well. I sat down beside her and we started to eat our pie.

"Are you still seeing that girl?" she asked, forking a bite into her mouth.

"Darcy?"

"Yeah."

"Not really," I said, looking down at the sand. "She's on tour for three months." The truth was that Darcy had broken up with me before she left and I was hoping she'd want to get back together when she returned.

"Oh." Willis stifled a smile and shifted in her pants. Then she looked at me slyly. "So, we're monogamous then?"

I knew it was at least partially a joke, but I felt unreasonably annoyed. "What makes you say that?" I tried to keep the edge out of my voice.

"I'm just kidding." She took another big bite of pie and looked intensely out at the ocean. "Did I ever tell you about that girl I knew in Regina?" She started to regale me with tales from her past, how she had this woman in a hot tub, that one in a tent during a wind storm; how her boss, twenty years her senior, had one day presented her with a round-trip ticket to Ireland and a gold bracelet along with a letter professing her undying passion.

I looked down at her newly-shined black shoes, then back up at her face before interrupting her. "Why are you dressed up? Is this a special day or something?"

She looked hurt, and then looked out at the waves. She carefully set her unfinished pie on the log beside her and turned to me, gazing into my eyes. "It's our one month anniversary," she said.

I was shocked. We had in no way codified our connection by giving it any sort of name. I called her "my date" because that was the only language available that somewhat matched what it was we were doing, but I had already decided that she would never be my girlfriend, and I squirmed away from calling her "my lover." It was too tender, too intimate. How could we have an anniversary if we hadn't even acknowledged we were in a relationship? I shifted uncomfortably and looked at the cigarette butts littering the sand at my feet. On the neighbouring log, someone had stacked stones on top of each other to make a sculpture. The waves lurched back and threw themselves at the shore.

Finally, I looked at her. In her eyes, I saw my reflection, my sunglasses and still mouth. I looked deeper and saw her sorrow and neediness and hurt. There was an angry set to her jaw. I wondered how she would punish me for not caring as much as she did.

She turned away abruptly and stiffly got up, picking up her jacket and holding it at her waist. She made a point of looking away from me, as if she didn't want me to see her face. She started to walk back toward the car. I had the sense that an elaborately planned seduction was wilting in her mind as she walked, and I felt disappointed. I picked up her half-eaten pie and my own and followed her through the sand.

Back in the car, she turned on the radio and hummed along as if nothing had happened. She kept her jacket crumpled in her lap. She said she'd have to drop me off earlier than planned because her roommate needed the car. She wanted to know if I was busy later in the week and if she could cook me dinner. Her motorcycle would be out of the shop and she could take me for a ride. I stumbled out a "yes," thinking of the barely suppressed anger in her eyes.

When she pulled up in front of my apartment, she didn't get out to open the door for me. She gave me a hurried kiss and sped away before I finished letting myself in.

That night, I dreamt I was married to a chubby, bearded young man who resembled my father. He came home from work in a bad mood, setting his briefcase on the floor without saying anything. I motherishly tried to soothe him, patting his arm, helping him out of his jacket. But my real feeling was that I wanted him to fuck me. And then he was fucking me and it was really good. But then I was the man, and I was fucking Willis from behind. Then she was on her knees in front of me. I was wearing her sparkly silver cock. I had the sense that I had chosen it because it was silly and playful; it proved it was all just fun and games. But as she started to take it into her mouth, I looked down and was caught by her green eyes. They were glassy with tears.

I woke up with a start. The room was stuffy, full of late-morning sun. My stomach hurt and my mouth was dry. The alarm beeped loudly from the bedside. I rolled over and turned it off.

There was a voicemail from Willis rather than her usual text. She had called sometime in the night while I was sleeping. Her tone was studied, both contrite and cheerful. She was very sorry to be cancelling our date. She wouldn't be able to take me out on her motorcycle, she said, and she knew I had been looking forward to that. But she had double-booked. She wondered if she could take me out for brunch the following weekend. She would like to meet up earlier but she was going to be super busy over the next couple of weeks because she had visitors from out of town. She hoped I would understand.

I did understand. This was the call I had been waiting for. I didn't know I had been waiting for it, but I had. I felt a surge of relief. The sunlight through the blinds made stripes across the blanket. I traced them with my fingers. I was free again. Free. But with this thought came another feeling, heavy, like an ache in my ribs.

I rolled over on my back and held the phone to my ear. I played the message again. I could hear the strain in her voice more clearly the second time.

A SNAKE IN THE GRASS

It was Tuesday and she was babysitting her sister's daughter Juniper, who hated going down for naps. The poor girl had a cold—again. Shannon was sitting on the couch in the late afternoon sun, trying to rock her to some sort of sleep or calm, but Juniper wouldn't close her eyes and Shannon's arms were getting tired.

"Sometimes at night a bear hugs me," Juniper said, looking intently into Shannon's eyes.

Shannon's heart clenched. "A bear?" she asked, trying to keep her voice neutral.

"A bear hugs me," Juniper repeated solemnly.

The familiar nausea rose up in Shannon's throat. She tried to read Juniper's expression but her brown eyes were strangely opaque and her mouth revealed no emotion. She felt something pulse under the surface of Juniper's soft pale skin. What was it? What was hiding there?

"Can I have some juice?" Juniper asked. She smiled.

"Sure, honey, sure." Shannon set Juniper down and distract-edly went into the kitchen to pour her some orange juice.

Her own daughters, Kelsey and Fiona, were sleeping snuggly in the next room, like two layers of a pink-and-red cake in their shared bunk bed. They were great nappers, her girls—almost never complained about bedtime, seemed to enjoy drifting off into their own secret land of castles, fairies, and ponies.

But Juniper had never liked to sleep, at least not at Shannon's house. She often threw a tantrum when Shannon tried to put her down, and Shannon often gave up trying and just fed her juice and crackers in the living room while the girls slept.

Come to think of it, Juniper's tantrums were becoming more frequent. It had been Kelsey's turn to choose a book for story time this afternoon, but when Juniper saw Kelsey running from her bedroom holding *The Three Little Bears*, she had angrily started to wail.

Hurrying from the kitchen, her hands wet from washing dishes, Shannon wasn't sure what had happened. "Did Kelsey accidentally hit you with the book?" she asked. "Kelsey, did you hit Juniper?"

Before Shannon could get an answer, Juniper grabbed the book, a furious expression on her face, and threw it behind the couch. Kelsey hit her in response and Shannon had to put them in separate corners of the living room with two different books while she quietly read *Frog and Toad* to Fiona on the couch.

There was no doubt about it: Juniper was an angry little girl. Much angrier than Shannon's daughters had ever been. Often she screamed for no reason and she had crying jags that some-times lasted for half an hour. Shannon knew children were given to extreme emotions, but she had never witnessed anything like this. Perhaps it was simply Juniper's personality.

Shannon felt that her sister, Jillian, neglected the child. Some-times, when Shannon ran her fingers through Juniper's hair, she found knots hiding under the smooth, brown surface and she had to get her small comb and carefully untangle them. Sometimes Jillian only fed her toast for breakfast and Shannon had to make Juniper up some eggs when she arrived. Juniper was known to snack on pop tarts and popsicles, even though Shannon had told her sister many times that sugar was poison. And then there was the matter of Jillian working full-time. Shan-non had chosen to stay home with her daughters so that they wouldn't be left with strangers who would teach them God knows what. But her sister insisted on returning to work ("My career," she called it—even the words annoyed Shannon. They sounded so pretentious. Why didn't she just say "my job"?) as a registrar after a mere six months, and so little Juniper was left in daycare or with her father when he was off work from his fish-ing boat. This is why Shannon had volunteered to watch her on Tuesdays, to assure that the girl would get some good, steady care, even if only for nine or ten hours a week.

Maybe Juniper's anger wasn't abnormal. Shannon's sponsor had often told her that anger was a natural emotion, bound to come up on her journey through the twelve steps. "Don't suppress it, but don't act on it either," Violet had counselled during their first meet-up at Common Grounds. They had sat side by side on one of the musty brown couches, spilling their coffees when they tried to steady the rickety table. Violet studied one of the ugly abstract oil paintings on the wall as if it were the face of an old friend. "Try to just be with it, watch it and let it pass." That first meeting, Violet had loaned her a book on anger written by a Buddhist monk who had become famous in the West. Violet said the book had really helped her, but Shannon found it nearly impossible to read. His tone was condescending, she felt. He advised that one should hold one's anger like a baby, cradle it and love it. Don't punch a pillow, he cautioned. You will only be rehearsing your anger and making it stronger. Don't run off and think of something else, don't drink a glass of water to calm yourself, he said. This will only suppress your anger and then it will rear up later, even more strongly.

At the time, Shannon thought his book was the stupidest bunch of opinions she had ever heard. It made no sense to her, and she had resented Violet for giving her the book. Only a few months into her recovery, she was often so angry that she punched walls and bit pillows. She even bit her own arms and slapped her own face. In fact, the book on anger had made her so angry that, while reading a particularly annoying passage in bed one night, she hurled it across the room. In the morning, she found it splayed on the floor, spine bent. She had picked it up, smoothed the cover, and returned it to Violet at the next meeting. "Thank you," she had said. "The book was very helpful."

Yet, years later, she had thought of the monk's words and thought he was probably right. When she had punched walls, she had only hurt her hands and made her apartment look like some trashed drug den. She had to wear long-sleeved shirts after biting her arms, even in hot weather, and this made her feel stupid and ashamed. She had never managed to see her anger as a little baby, but she had finally managed to stop punching walls and screaming. It took years, though.

Shannon returned to the living room with Juniper's juice. The girl was slumped on the couch, staring passively off into space. Shannon again felt her heart shift painfully in her chest. What had the girl seen? What had happened to her? Was the bear just a nightmare?

Shannon sat down carefully beside her. She thought about holding the juice for Juniper while she drank, but she wanted Juniper to know that she trusted her not to dump it all over the couch, so she handed it to her, wrapping both of Juniper's hands around the cup. "Be careful like a big girl, okay, honey? Don't spill."

Juniper sucked down the juice and Shannon strained to hear sounds of her daughters stirring in the next room. She didn't hear anything. She placed her hands on her knees and tried to appear calm.

"Does the bear scare you?" she asked gently.

Juniper stared back uncomprehendingly.

"The bear who hugged you?" Shannon wrapped her arms around herself to mime a hug. She rocked back and forth a little before realizing that this comforting motion was not the one she wanted to make. She stopped and dropped her hands into her lap. "The bear you were telling me about?"

Juniper slurped up the last of her juice and clutched the cup between her hands. She looked at Shannon with her big eyes. "No," she said. "More juice?"

Just then a crash resounded in the next room and Kelsey screamed. Something large hit the wall and there was muffled scuffling. "I am NOT the princess!" Fiona screeched. Shannon hurried to check on her daughters, leaving Juniper alone with her empty cup.

That night, after she put her daughters to bed, reading them two stories and tucking their favourite stuffed animals under the covers with them, she poured herself a cup of very strong peppermint tea and put three whole-wheat honey cookies on a plate. Then she called her other sister, Bethany. Bethany didn't have any children. She was an actress, but she called herself an actor. She liked it to be known that she had never waited tables, but that she had done a hell of a lot of administrative work for various theatre and dance companies. In between shows, she liked to say. Something's got to pay the bills, she liked to say. I'm a numbers person *and* a people person, she often said.

Shannon was usually in a fight with one of her sisters. Most recently, it had been Bethany. But last week they had gone out for Thai food, Shannon had given Bethany a new mystery novel, and the evening had ended with the two of them commiserating about how Jillian never seemed to have time for either of them since she went back to work. They'd shared a long good-bye hug and promised to call each other more.

Before Bethany could finish her hello, Shannon started speaking. "Bethy, I have to talk to you about something." Shannon's tone implied that she was about to disclose secrets that could only be shared with this one sister.

Shannon quickly explained the situation. There was a heavy silence on the other end of the line. Shannon assumed Bethany was as shocked and scared as she had been that afternoon. Bethany had a very sensitive temperament. Shannon took a big gulp of her tea and listened for sounds of crying, but didn't hear any. The silence lengthened. Finally, Shannon broke it. "We have to get Juniper out of that house."

Bethany roused herself. "Shouldn't you talk to Jillian first? I mean..." She paused, as if thinking about how to best phrase her next words.

"She'll deny it, of course!" Shannon snapped. "If I have to do this alone, I will. I just thought you might care enough to want to save your niece."

Bethany breathed a sigh into the phone. "Of course I care about Juniper. I just don't know if what she told you is really that much cause for worry. I mean, I used to be afraid of cats." Bethany laughed. "Children are easily scared of weird things."

Shannon wished she had a pillow to punch. She took an angry bite of her cookie and chewed it loudly in Bethany's ear. When she finally spoke, she didn't attempt to keep the ice out of her voice. "Well, thanks for nothing. Thanks for absolutely nothing."

"Shan—wait," Bethany said. "Just hold on a minute. Do you really think Jillian wouldn't notice if there was something going on? And Paul, I mean..."

"Jillian!" Shannon heard her voice rising. "Jillian couldn't protect anyone!" Her hands were shaking so hard she could barely hold the phone. Before Bethany could say anything else, she hung up.

She stared at the two cookies and wished she could pick up the plate and hurl it against the wall. She wished she could scream until her lungs hurt. But just down the hall her daughters were sleeping, and besides, the new Shannon didn't scream anymore.

She took the plate of cookies and her mug of tea to the living room. She noticed her hands were still shaking as she set the mug down on the coffee table. She pulled the tattered quilt that lived on the back of the couch around her and snuggled into the cushions, even though she wasn't cold. Patrick was working late again. But even if he was home, she knew he would have no patience for her story. He had told her during their last counselling session that he didn't want to hear anything else about her fights with her sisters. "It's your business," he had said. "Keep me out of it."

Now she was fighting with Bethany again. She felt a twinge of embarrassment, but quickly squelched it. It wasn't her fault. Bethany had acted in her usual selfish manner. Shannon didn't know why she'd expected anything else. But maybe Bethany couldn't help it. Maybe all actresses, or actors, were selfish. They saved the best of themselves for the stage and had nothing left for their human relationships. They didn't understand real, everyday problems. They lacked life skills, these actors, living in one or another fantasy world of frilly costumes and silly accents, and drinks after the show, revelling in boisterous and shallow conversations with other empty people who tried to act their way through life.

Or maybe it was because Bethany wasn't a mother. She just couldn't understand what it meant to love another more than herself. She wouldn't die for anyone. She didn't have the same protective instinct. Bethany didn't understand the feeling that you could kill someone just for looking at your child the wrong way. Jillian did. Or so she had said, more than once, to Shannon. But Jillian had gotten so busy the last couple of years. Like their mother, who was always working, always waiting for a bus to carry her to one of her two jobs, or at the all-night grocery store after one of her shifts trying to get them something to eat. Their mother, who had to leave Jillian and Shannon alone with their father. The father Bethany hadn't even known because he died before she turned one.

Afraid of cats! She had laughed! Shannon pictured Bethany's face laughing and she wanted to slap it. She caught herself. No, she didn't want to slap her. Maybe she wanted to grab her shoulders and shake her a little bit. Maybe tell her very clearly and emphatically that she was wrong. But not slap her. That was the old Shannon. The new Shannon didn't hit things or people anymore. The new Shannon had never hit her children. That was something she was very proud of. She would never be capable of hurting a child.

Shannon imagined Juniper's round little face, the crease of her double chin, her huge brown eyes. Kelsey and Fiona had picked out a stuffed bear for her last Christmas and Juniper had loved it, had carried it around all day on her hip, burping it like a baby over her shoulder. What had happened to it? Could it be the bear Juniper was talking about? But no, that was ridiculous. That bear was much smaller than Juniper. It couldn't hug her.

Juniper's father Paul was a big, dark-haired man with a bushy beard and hairy knuckles. He wore dark flannel shirts and jeans and his laugh was deep and raspy at the edges, almost like a growl. Shannon had always found him a bit too large, a bit too friendly. And, though she had never admitted it to Jillian, she was afraid of him. She would never have married a man like him.

The first time Paul had come to pick up Juniper, he had looked intently into Shannon's eyes when he said thank you and held her hand for too long when they shook goodbye. And then there were his inappropriate jokes. The last time she had seen him, he had cracked one about a drunk priest. And although the joke didn't mention children, she had wondered if that was the subtext. And why had Paul told a joke about drinking anyway, when he knew she was in recovery? It was weird. It was more than weird. It was alarming. Paul had laughed his growly laugh and tried to meet her eyes, but she had coldly looked away to let him know she didn't appreciate his humour.

Patrick rarely made jokes. He was lean and sensitive and quiet. He was exactly her height, and his well-groomed hands were more delicate than hers. He programmed computers for a living. She had never heard him yell. When his daughters screamed, he would look at her and then leave the room to read his newspaper. Or, if he was in a tolerant mood, he would put his hands over his ears and quietly say, "I can't hear you unless you use a normal tone." She sometimes felt like she was raising the kids by herself.

Shannon felt another surge of anger. She thought of Bethany's calm, measured voice. Maybe Bethany was right. Maybe she was overreacting. She stood up abruptly and started walking around the room, clutching the quilt to her chest. She circled for what felt like a long time, and finally found herself stopped in front of the tall bookshelf in the corner. The shelf was crammed with children's books, novels, and computer manuals; one spine, thin and glittery, stood out from the rest.

During one of their first meetings, Violet, had told her to "write stuff down." "It will seriously help you," she had said, tucking her bleached blond hair behind her ear and taking a deep sip of her black coffee. "Get a journal and start writing down your feelings. My sponsor told me to do it when I first started and it totally works." After their meeting, Shannon had gone to the drugstore next door and bought a notebook with blue metallic butterflies on it and a pack of blue ballpoint pens. For a few weeks, she had sat down every few days to diligently record her thoughts and feelings. She told the people at the meetings about the notebook, and they said encouraging things about her ability to understand her own actions, about emotional intelligence, and taking responsibility. But she never found the practice of writing things down particularly interesting or helpful, and after awhile, she stopped bothering to do it. What was the point, she wondered. Feelings were to be had and forgotten. Writing them down didn't help her to understand them better. When she read over her journal entries, they just seemed like a bunch of disembodied black words floating on white-lined paper. The only thing she had learned from the exercise was that she didn't like her handwriting much.

But now she couldn't call Bethany; she couldn't talk to Patrick. The girls were too little and it wouldn't be appropriate to talk to them about it anyway.

She pulled the journal from the shelf and went into the kitchen, rooting through her miscellaneous drawer until she found a pen. Then she went back to the couch. Her tea was cold so she drank it down quickly like water. She had no appetite for the cookies. They stared out at her from the white plate like two blank eyes.

She opened the notebook. An entry dated nine years prior told her that she had wished she was dead that day, that she had eaten half a pint of strawberry cheesecake ice cream, and that she was fat and stupid and she hoped Patrick wouldn't call her when she was feeling so horrible because she might yell at him. Had she really thought that? She tried to avoid reading any other words as she flipped through, looking for the first blank page. She grasped the pen. It was sweaty in her hand. She tentatively set the tip down on the paper.

And then she was drawing—spirals and circles and viney flowers and lopsided stars, squares upon squares became buildings with moons peeking out of their windows. And then tall trees and below the trees, tall grasses, and then a very long snake. A snake. She stopped and set the pen down beside her on the couch. Her hands were shaking again, harder now. She felt nauseous. She thought of her niece's sweet, soft, pale face. She thought of the almost maniacal pitch of her screams. The girl was troubled. And here she was drawing rather than doing anything about it.

She closed the notebook and grasped it with both hands. She wanted to tear it apart like it was a limbed creature who had fatally bitten someone she loved. She wanted to kill it. But it was just paper. She let it slip from her hands and fall to the floor. She felt like stabbing out her eyes and crying. Something fluttered out from between the pages and landed on the green rug. She bent down to pick it up.

It was a card with a picture of a cat on the front. The cat was a grey tabby, and it was climbing up a flight of stairs. Light poured from the top, as if the stairs ended in an open door to a room that housed the sun. At the bottom of the card were the words "One Day At A Time" written in gold cursive letters.

Shannon remembered the day Jillian had given her the card. Jillian had surprised her with a party at her apartment on the one-year anniversary of her sobriety. There had been an ice cream cake and sparkling apple juice and balloons, Patrick in a bowtie, Bethany and her new girlfriend, Violet and a few acquaintances from the program. They had sat in a circle on Shannon's living room floor and made awkward conversation. After about an hour, everyone but Patrick went home, hugging and congratulating her as they left. At the door, Jillian squeezed her, burrowing her face into Shannon's brown curls. "I'm so proud of you," she said. These were the same words she had written inside the card she had left on the table next to the melting remains of the cake.

Although Patrick had told her she shouldn't have been, Shannon was furious. Proud of her! As if she was some child who had completed her first hopscotch without falling. As if she had just brought home a good report card. Jillian was only two years older than her. She was in no position to be proud of anything Shannon had done, especially since she had gotten sober without one iota of Jillian's help.

And to make it worse: One Day At A Time! As if Jillian knew anything about that. Jillian barely ever drank. Even in high school she had been the goodie two-shoes who hung out with the honour roll kids in the cafeteria while Shannon smoked dope and drank peach coolers in older boys' cars parked beyond the football field. As an adult, Jillian occasionally sipped at a glass of white wine while out to dinner, but she was just as likely to order sparkling water. She knew nothing about how hard it was to take it one day at a time, how hard those first few months had been.

Yet Shannon had kept the card.

She opened it slowly, almost expecting it to creak like the hinge of an old box. Jillian had used a green pen. Shannon had forgotten that detail. She had printed her words carefully, dotting her i's with circles, an affectation she had picked up in high school and never discarded. Shannon's eyes glanced over the words, not really taking them in. Then she slowed down to actually read them. Underneath "I'm so proud of you," Jillian had written, "My dear sister."

She had forgotten that part. Dear.

Dear sister.

She let the card fall to the floor. She looked again at the cookies, the blank face of the plate. She suddenly felt nauseous again. Her throat muscles tightened. In the notebook on the floor were the pictures she had doodled to try to get in touch with her emotions. And what she had gotten in touch with was that same old snake. "The snake in the grass," her father had called it. "The snake wants to make friends." "The snake has come out to play." She put her hand to her throat. She was going to be sick.

When her sister had come to pick up Juniper that evening, Shannon had all of Juniper's things, her books and her stuffed kangaroo and her dirty clothes, packed into her little turquoise backpack. She had stood at the door and handed it to Jillian without a word. She did this so Jillian would not try to come inside like she usually did, would not try to share a cup of tea or find out how Shannon's day had been, if she had any funny stories about Juniper or the girls. She wanted Jillian to realize right away that this was not a night for small talk, that she had discovered what Jillian, frazzled and distracted by her all-important career, had been too oblivious to see. She held out the backpack to her sister as if it might contain an explosive device. "Your daughter told me something today," she had said coldly. "We need to talk."

And Shannon remembered the look on Jillian's face, her eyebrows rising in worry over brown eyes already filling with hurt and surprise, her face tensed in anticipation.

SEEKER

Ron kisses her on the cheek, warm breath, lips lingering for a moment. Then he climbs up into the cab of his old blue truck and starts the engine. It rattles and chokes; the truck lurches forward and he waves goodbye.

She is alone. Snow all around her, and at the bottom of the slope, a small creek, not yet frozen, a cardinal on an iced branch upon which a few frosted red berries still cling.

The cabin is in better shape than she expected. Small, she knew that, but well-constructed, the worn grey logs snug against each other. Inside, it is spare, clean, no curtains on the windows, a simple wooden table, one chair, a wood stove. Julie leans her pack against the wall and climbs up the ladder to the loft. The foam mattress is covered in a patchwork quilt and she wraps herself in it, lying down to look out the small diamond-shaped window at the pines, the white mountains rising above.

His wife has never been here. This is his refuge, only his; he spends several weeks of every year here.

And he has kindly let her use it for this month. She didn't even have to ask—he just offered one night after meditation group. She was walking out the door, talking with Susan, and he walked up behind them.

"A retreat?" he asked. "You know I have that cabin up north?"

She turned to him. In fact she had forgotten about the cabin, although he had told her about it once.

"I'm not going up this December. Family stuff." He smiled wryly. "So you're free to use it, if you want."

Susan had smiled that discrete smile of hers and looked down at the ground. Julie thought the smile meant Susan was shy because she knew about their affair, knew it had ended a couple of months before, and didn't want it to be awkward for either of them.

Julie looked at Ron's face, browned from a summer outdoors. He looked thinner, his smile lines and the wrinkles on his forehead more pronounced. His white hair stuck straight up, as usual, but she noticed it was shaved close to the skin above either ear; he must have recently gotten a haircut. It was good to see him taking care of himself again.

"I can drive you there," he continued. "In late November, first week of December."

Susan tapped her foot on the ground. They might miss their bus if the conversation continued.

"Sure," Julie said. "I mean, I'll call you."

When she said yes, she wasn't sure she had meant it. But then everything fell into place: her boss gave her the month off because it was the slow season and his daughter would be back from college to help with the restaurant, Susan agreed to water her plants, her sister loaned her a down coat, and her AA sponsor gave her some sturdy boots. She had enough money in savings to buy the food and supplies she needed. The only thing that didn't fall into place was Mel.

"You're going to his cabin now? Seriously?" They were on the phone, and Mel puffed a bit as she talked—she must have been walking up the hill to her house. "I bet he tries to stay there with you. 'Oops! I forgot—I planned to do a meditation retreat now too. Guess we'll just have to do it together.' Or else he drops you off and then shows up the next day for a 'visit,' saying he forgot an important book or something." Mel heaved a disdainful sigh into the phone.

Mel had never liked Ron. When she found out Julie was seeing him, her first words were: "What are you trying to do? Fuck your father? It's so cliché."

Mel hadn't said she was mad at Julie for dating a man, but Julie knew that was at least part of the reason. Another part was that Mel thought Ron was an old perv. Julie had made the mistake of telling Mel that Ron had dated some of the other women in the meditation group. Just two that she knew of, which in her mind didn't make him a lech. Although both of the women, like her, were significantly younger than him.

"*And* he's married," Mel had pointed out in a disgusted tone.

Julie had tried to explain about Ron and Muriel's open relationship, about their no-jealousy policy, about the dinner they had all shared and the loaf of bread Muriel had baked for her when Ron told her they had started dating.

Mel hadn't bought it. She'd sat at Julie's kitchen table, her arms crossed. Then she'd uncrossed them to run her finger across her plate and lick up the extra tomato sauce. Smacking her lips, she'd made her final pronouncement: "He's a sleeze."

Mel hated it when people she considered "serious lesbians" dated men ("cis-gendered men," she would always clarify). Also, she had once, long ago, been Julie's girlfriend.

Out the window, white wispy clouds race over the mountains. Soon it will be getting dark. She should get up and scoop some snow to melt for water. Rice for dinner tonight. But all she wants to do is lie here. She doesn't know why she's so tired. She didn't do much today—got up, drank coffee, waited for Ron to arrive, packed up the truck, drove up here.

Maybe it was being around Ron that tired her. The subtle neediness—not apparent in group—that leaks out of him when they are alone. His gaze burrowing into hers, his sensitive questions, his soft touch on her leg or arm. These are the things she doesn't miss. Although she does miss him sometimes. Not the sex, but the conversations, the quiet time spent together cooking, reading, walking. They had only dated for six months. But it had felt longer. It had been a novelty, dating a man, especially one so much older than her. But once the novelty wore off, she was bored.

The thing was, dating him made her want to drink. Even early on, the second or third week, she found herself thinking "I should get a bottle of wine to go with this pasta" or "Maybe he'll bring a six pack of IPA." Biking through the industrial district after work, it was all she could do not to stop at one of the microbreweries bubbling with conversation and laughter, the smell of fermenting hops heavy in the air. She was sure she saw an old friend in the group smoking out front, someone with auburn hair or a black mohawk. Someone in torn jeans or a half-shirt that showed her navel ring. Remember how his moustache used to dip into his pint? Remember how she used to try to take everyone's shirt off when she got really drunk? It was always so hilarious. It made her nostalgic. And nostalgia was one step from relapse, she knew. The possibility of relapsing made her angry, and she turned the anger on Ron, although he hadn't really done anything, had he?

He took it very well. They had been cuddling together on her couch and he sat up with a sudden urgency, asking, "We'll still be friends, right? You'll still come to group?" There was a desperate tone to his questions, as if he feared he might never see her again. And what of it? What if he never saw her again? He had dozens of friends. He had a good job. He had a wife. He had a cabin all of his own up in the woods.

After they broke up, she still wanted to drink. And that was when she got really worried.

It was once again difficult—as it had been the first several months—to serve drinks to customers. She jealously watched them sip gin and tonics, slurp up mimosas. A couple of times her anxiety caused her to upset a tray of frosty beers and her boss glared at her.

Her co-workers were always sitting in the bar after their shifts, having a few before heading home. She hadn't been tempted to join them for many months, but now she had to will herself out the door and onto her bike. She started taking a different route home so she wouldn't pass the microbreweries. She tried to keep herself busy. She called Mel for dinner dates, her sponsor for coffee dates. She started going to meetings in the morning before her shifts. But listening to middle-aged people talk about how hard it was to stay sober only annoyed her and made her want to go to a bar and pound back a number of whisky and sodas.

It was after a few weeks of this that she started thinking about doing a retreat. Ron, who led the meditation group, had done a lot of them and always recommended them to others, with the warning that they "weren't for the light of heart."

Ron had once been an ordained Buddhist monk, had spent many years in a monastery in Japan before he met and married Muriel. It was one of the things that made him so attractive. The calmness he radiated, his slow way of talking, his ability to be silent for long periods of time.

He had something she wanted and she thought that if she got close enough to him she might catch it, like a benign virus. But of course she knew it didn't work that way—had always known it, on some level. She had learned it before with different people, but apparently she had to play out the lesson again with Ron.

But hadn't it all been a sham, anyway? He wasn't, after all, really that peaceful, when it came down to it. He could be petty, passive-aggressive. Sometimes he called her just to gossip about the other members of the group; sometimes he snapped at her or pretended not to hear her questions when he was upset. When they were in bed, it often took him a long time to get it up, and he acted like he was doing her a favour when he went down on her.

Her plan before coming to the cabin was to meditate and do yoga in the morning, take a long walk after lunch, and meditate again in the evening. For the first few days, she follows this schedule, although it's hell to stay sitting on her mat. Her back aches, she fidgets, she can't calm her mind. By the fourth day, she gives up her routine. Instead she washes the inside of the windows, drying them so they won't ice up. She mops the floor on her hands and knees. She chops the firewood—already chopped by Ron—into smaller pieces. She takes out her phone and looks at it; it's dead. She goes outside to feel how cold it is. She puts on layers of clothing and takes them off. She stokes the fire. And finally, when there is nothing left to do, she climbs back up the ladder to wrap herself in the quilt and lie for hours looking out the window.

Next to the bed, there is a small ledge nailed into the wall. On it are a few books—*The Power of Now, Be Here Now, Start Where You Are,* the *Tao Te Ching.* She chooses the last title because it seems the least aggressive. It's not telling her what to do and it doesn't have the word "power" in it. She flips through it. A number of the passages are underlined in dark blue ink; others are highlighted in bright orange. There are notes in two different handwritings on nearly every page. She quickly shuts the book, feeling like she has stumbled upon someone's diary. Do the notes belong to Ron? Or did he get the book at a used bookstore, with the writing already in it?

She sets the book back on the shelf and lies back to look out the window. The sky is blue again, free of clouds, the mountains a glistening hard white. The pines shift in the wind. A hawk soars by.

The blue notes are definitely his. She recognizes his handwriting. That means the highlighted passages and the notes in black must be from someone else. Muriel? Who else could it be? Unless he was responding to notes that were already written in the book when he bought it.

Julie sits back up and pulls the book off the shelf, opening it gingerly. She's on page sixty-nine. Ha. She only got him to try it once. He claimed it was too awkward, too uncomfortable. Uncomfortable. Yet he had no problem with her bruising her knees on the hardwood when she kneeled for so long in front of him.

The passage on page sixty-nine reads:

I have three treasures which I hold and keep.
The first is mercy; the second is economy;
the third is daring not to be ahead of others.
From mercy comes courage; from economy comes generosity;
From humility comes leadership.

Next to this last line, in blocky, blue print, Ron had written: "But only if it's *real* humility. Fake humility can never produce a good leader."

Underneath this, in curlicues of black ink, are two questions: "But how can you tell if it's fake? What if a leader tricks herself or himself into believing their humility is genuine?"

"Self-knowledge is the only worthy pursuit," Ron had written under this, in even bigger letters, as if the sheer size of his print settled the argument.

And Muriel, or whoever it was, had not bothered to reply.

Julie flips to another page. Only one line is highlighted orange. "He who grasps loses." Next to it, the black scrawl reads: "When I grasp, I am not myself." Underneath this, Ron's blocky letters: "And yet, what better thing to grasp for than spiritual truth?"

The black handwriting replies: "The Tao is like water—it can't be grasped (see pg. 23)."

"Yet it is also very 'real' (see also pg. 23)—and this is what we must strive to live, the real-ness of this essence" retorts the blue print.

Under this, the black handwriting reads simply: "You are talking in circles."

Julie closes the book. She can see now it is a record of more than their spiritual arguments. They are not really arguments, after all. They are code for something deeper—some deeply shared agreement. That they could even write these things to each other.

She lies back down, the book resting on her belly. Why had Ron lied about Muriel coming here? She must have come here. It's such a beautiful place, so full of the quiet they both love.

And if he lied about that, what else had he lied about?

He had told her that he and Muriel no longer had sex. Muriel was in a new phase of her life—"a stage on her path," is how Ron described it—in which she no longer desired sex. At first, Ron told Julie, he had believed he too could enter a period of celibacy, perhaps even stay there for the rest of his life. But within a few months, he realized that wasn't possible. And that's when he started sleeping with women in the group.

Only two of them. Well, three, counting her. Unless he had lied about that too.

And what did it matter if he lied about it? What if he slept with all of them, what if he is still sleeping with Muriel?

She realizes, suddenly, that she is very cold. The fire has died down and the down comforter is pushed to the bottom of the bed. The quilt isn't thick enough to keep her warm. She needs to get up and stoke the fire before the embers burn out, but what she really wants is a drink. A few gulps from a flask of Jack Daniels to warm her bones. A tall glass of merlot to sip while she reads one of the bedside books—maybe she'll start with *Start Where You Are*. Where She Is is freezing her ass off, smelling the rum and cinnamon of an imagined hot toddy.

She pulls the comforter over her. This is dangerous thinking. She knows that. They're dangerous, the thoughts she's found herself indulging in the last few weeks. The thoughts she came here to get away from. No, not get away from, she corrects herself. Look at. Look at closely and transform.

Yes, she has relapsed. Once. Twice. The bartender at work had made a mistake margarita and was going to pour it down the sink, and Julie offered to give it to a favourite customer—but instead she snuck in the back and chugged it in the walk-in fridge.

The next week she took her old route home, and instead of cruising past the first microbrewery, she found herself braking, locking her bike and going inside to sit alone at the bar, the blare of drunken conversation warming her back as she drank ruby ales and lagers and wheat beers until the place closed. Luckily she knew enough to walk her bike home, but she can't really remember the rest of the night—except that she woke up at some early hour, her stomach a clenched fist, bile rising in her throat, and had to race to the bathroom before she puked all over her bed.

But there is nothing to drink here, except water melted from snow. There is nothing to read, except these few books. And the darkness coming on.

What is she doing here, lying in bed, daydreaming? She should be meditating. But the thought of it makes her want to curl up in a ball and cry. She knows she can't afford to begin any sort of slide into depression. What if she stopped eating? She imagines Ron finding her emaciated corpse wrapped up in the quilt, the *Tao Te Ching* open beside her to some poignant passage. The image is so self-indulgent that it makes her laugh in spite of herself. Really, the only thing she might die of up here is boredom.

She flings off the comforter and quilt. Time to take a walk.

Outside, the air is crisp, a trace smell of branches frozen in ice. It snowed all night, and there is at least a foot of fresh snow on the ground. She tromps toward a path in the woods, hoping the uphill trek will wake her up, make her more motivated to meditate.

Her phone is dead, and she didn't bring a watch, so she never knows the exact time, but she guesses it can't be later than three. Still, the woods are already heavy with the shadows of dusk. She keeps thinking she sees a person, a shape lurking—but it's just the trees and their shadows. She chants a mantra, one that Ron taught the group. It calms her mind, even as her breath quickens as she chugs uphill, the snow up to her knees.

She comes to a break in the trees and pauses. She smells the strong musky smell of urine and looks down to see an indentation in the snow near her feet. She steps closer, peering into the dark yellow crevasse. Beyond it are large footprints burned into the snow, trailing off into the woods. For a moment, she is too amazed to be afraid. After four days of solitude, it seems magical, this sight. That other creatures exist, are walking the earth right here next to her.

But then she comes back to her senses. The sensible thing is to be afraid. She looks around. Pine branches laden with snow, bushes that look like large white cakes. Silence. There are shadows, but she doesn't see any shape that could be a wolf or a cougar. A northern flicker swoops out from the trees; she catches the gleam of orange under its wing. She backs away slowly, looking in all directions, just in case.

Back in the cabin, she lights the two kerosene lamps and several candles. Darkness is nearly upon her, and with darkness comes the fear of it. It is the first time in her life she has really felt this fear. But then, in the city she always sleeps with a nightlight and she seldom sleeps alone—this is something Mel has criticized her for, this tendency toward serial relationships. These last couple of months are the first time in years that she has been single.

She decides that rather than hide in bed, she will meditate. She positions her cushion in front of the wood stove and wraps the quilt around her legs. Just an hour, one hour of sitting before she makes dinner.

She closes her eyes and almost immediately starts reproaching herself. What was she thinking, coming up here, alone, in December? It is so dark. So cold.

She remembers a story Ron told her about his first retreat, the winter after he bought the cabin. Forty days of snow and silence. Somewhere, about halfway through, he woke up in the middle of the night to the sound of dripping. He thought he'd left the faucet on, that the bathtub was overflowing—but then he remembered there was no running water, no bathtub. He threw the blankets off and climbed downstairs. And then he realized something. He wasn't cold. The room wasn't cold. And the dripping was coming from outside.

He opened the door and stepped onto the porch. Wet floorboards soaked into his wool socks. The foot of snow on the railing had disappeared. Water rolled off the roof. The ground was almost bare, just a few traces of white. How was this possible, he had wondered. Snow melting in the dead of winter?

The next morning, it was still warm and at sunrise a huge bank of clouds—"more like one big long cloud, a sort of blanket or carpet," he explained—lit up, a luxurious gold. "It was sort of like the fur of a fox, some stole a lady might wear," he told her. The contrast between the cloud and the sky—which was a deep morning blue—was magnificent, one of the most beautiful things he'd seen in his life.

"After I came back to the city, I was more calm. After having been in contact with that kind of beauty." He said this while lying on her couch, his head in her lap. She was stroking his white hair. It was one of the few times she had felt comfortable mothering him.

She is surprised by a pang of longing. She starts to squelch it, and then stops herself. There is something familiar about it, something she can't quite put her finger on.

It is so dark. So cold. If only she had just a little bit of whisky. Just a touch to sip on in front of the fire.

If only Mel was here, someone to talk to. If only sensible Susan. If only her sister, who always knows how to make her laugh.

Even Ron. If only Ron was here.

There is a crack from the fire. She opens her eyes to see sparks, a log snapping. It is only the fourth day of thirty. And she is only thirty. Thirty years old. The night is coming on and there is still so much time.

HIDER

I have been living at the monastery for just over seven months when the newcomer arrives. Rather than knock at the big wooden doors at the front of the building, he comes to the screened back-door, which I have left open to allow the steam to escape. I am alone in the kitchen, humming under my breath as I scrub the pots and bowls. Slowly, I become aware of some other, very sub-tle, vibration under my humming—as if an insect throbs nearby or someone across the kitchen is waving a fan. I turn to look and I see a tall man with long brown hair standing outside the screen door. He doesn't speak at first, but simply stares at me, and then raises his hand to knock on the frame.

The day is overcast, as it often is on the mountain, but the man is wearing dark sunglasses. I am not the jumpy sort, but some-thing about him makes me wish the door was shut and locked. I focus on my breathing, as Som has instructed us to do when we are feeling any emotion. Counting three in and three out breaths, I slowly walk to the screen door. "Can I help you?"

He doesn't lift his sunglasses, but pushes his hair back from his face in a friendly gesture. Up close, he seems almost ordinary, the kind of guy who whistles to himself at a bus stop, someone you might ignore or give a smoke to if you were feeling magnanimous. He wears a long baggy grey sweater, beat-up cargo pants, and worn sneakers. A backpack dangles from one of his hands; it's small, the size that elementary school children use, and grimy. His skin is a greenish white, with dry, flakey patches; his lips are chapped. He looks like he's been on the road for some time. He stifles a cough as he attempts to clear his throat. "Is this the Kanda Monastery?"

"Yes," I say, keeping my voice even. "But as you can see, this is the kitchen. Why don't you go around to the front door and the teacher will talk with you?"

My unfriendliness surprises me. I've been warming myself for some weeks with the idea that I have become a kinder person since arriving at the monastery.

He hesitates, a vague smile on his face. I wish he would lift his sunglasses so I could read his eyes. He sets his backpack down on the dirt at his feet. "The thing is, I can't see the teacher yet," he says. "I thought I'd take a shower and put on clean clothes and then go see him."

"You have clean clothes?"

He shifts as if to acknowledge either his own griminess or my insult. "I know someone here, I think."

"Who?"

"Rolf?" As if sensing my unasked question, he continues, "I know him from work. We used to work together on a farm." He shifts again, as if his loose clothing is constricting him.

"Rolf usually works on the labyrinth after the midday meal."
I point to a stand of evergreens. "On the other side of those trees,
you'll find him."

The stranger turns, tossing his small backpack over his shoulder, and starts walking away, but then turns back to me. "I'd like
to work in the kitchen," he says. I take in my image, reflected in
his sunglasses. I look serious, older than I am. "If the teacher
lets me stay, I mean. I'm a pretty good cook." He smiles as if it's
difficult to do so, and then rubs his hands together in a friendly
gesture that doesn't become him. "Curries, soups…" He looks
around, examining the trees lining the clearing, the laundry line
hung with dishtowels and a few shirts and socks. When I don't
respond, he hitches his backpack up further on his shoulder and
strolls determinedly towards the labyrinth.

The rest of the day, as I place one foot slowly in front of the
other, walking the paths through the forest, as I watch my breath
enter and leave my nostrils, I think of this strange newcomer,
and wonder who he is and why he's come here. Already, I have
a proprietary feeling about the monastery, as if part of it—the
kitchen, perhaps, some of the paths, and certainly my hut—belongs to me. Somchai has sensed this, and has already started
giving me lessons to lessen my attachment. Last week, he asked
me to switch huts, even though he knows I love mine—it's the
farthest away, the closest to the woods—with Rolf, whose hut is
nearer to the main hall. I complied because, after these many
months, I have learned to trust Som's suggestions.

When I enter the meditation hall that evening, the newcomer is already sitting there, his posture erect, chin bent slightly forward. He radiates a sort of fake humility, like he's acting some role— I don't know how else to explain it. Strangely, he is still wearing his sunglasses.

He has taken a cushion up front, closest to where Som usually sits. It is Suchart's spot. I feel a surge of annoyance seeing him there, but stifle it and take my place in the back row. Slowly the other monks file in. Suchart doesn't say anything to the stranger; he just takes another cushion and mat from the back of the hall and sets it next to me, then quietly positions himself and begins meditating.

I close my eyes to do the same, and then open them when I hear Som enter. Som shuffles over to the newcomer and bends down, putting a hand on his shoulder. He whispers something in his ear and the man nods, then takes off his sunglasses and sets them on the floor next to his mat.

After the meditation, Som clears his throat. "We have a new visitor," he tells us, gesturing at the stranger. "Mark. He will stay awhile. Help him feel at home." He smiles at each of us.

Mark turns from his cushion to look back at us, gives a strained smile, and waves one hand before turning back to face Som.

"He will help Rolf and John with the labyrinth for now," Som proclaims.

I can't see Mark's face, but I get the sense—something in his posture—that he is displeased with this assignment.

The next day I emerge from my walk in the woods to see Mark standing over John and Rolf as they crouch on the ground, arranging rocks. I can't hear what he's saying to them, but his tone is chastising. Rolf's shoulders are hunched defensively, but John's posture looks indifferent. I decide to fabricate a reason for joining them.

As I walk up, I hear Mark ask incredulously, "You don't know how long you've been working on it?"

John replies, "We don't know because it doesn't matter." Then he sees me and smiles. "Hi, Misaki."

Mark turns to look at me. It's the first time I've seen his eyes; they are unnerving, a flat black. His sunglasses are pushed up on top of his head and there is a red patch above his eyebrow that looks like it's recently been scratched. He blinks repeatedly, as if he isn't used to being in the light. "Can you believe how long they've been working on this?"

The fact is, John and Rolf have been constructing the labyrinth for months, and they only have a couple of circles completed. They dismantled it and started over several times. Some rocks have been discarded; others cracked in half, still others repainted. I know little about the project other than the occasional story they share over evening tea, but their process appears to be very involved, including much consultation with each other and with Som. It's difficult for anyone to say when the labyrinth will be done—or if finishing it is even the goal—but Som seems satisfied with their progress.

"A labyrinth isn't difficult to build. It's just some rocks in the dirt. First you make your plan, and then you execute it. Remember the one on the farm, Rolf? It couldn't have taken them more than a week."

Rolf stares silently at the dirt. I notice he has a star shaved over his right ear. He and John are the only two people here who still shave their heads.

Mark rubs his hands together. "So let's make a goal. Next Tuesday—a week. In a week's time, this thing will be done."

I decide it's time to interrupt. "Mark, are you allergic to anything? Tep and I are planning next week's menu."

Mark looks at me coldly. "I like eggs and fish."

"No allergies?"

"None."

I don't bother to tell him that we don't eat animals here. He will figure that out soon enough.

The next day, I arrive to prepare the midday meal to find the fridge door sagging open and Mark rummaging through the cupboards over the sink. The room is chillier than usual. Mark is wearing two sweaters, one on top of the other, and a wool hat.

"What are you looking for?" I ask.

"Salt," he says. "We can't make the stew without it."

"We don't keep salt in the fridge." I close the door. "And Tep and I are making stir-fry today."

Tep walks in just as I utter his name. He looks at Mark questioningly.

Mark gives him a tight smile. "I've been transferred to kitchen duty. Somchai's orders."

I guessed as much. Som wouldn't tolerate Mark's bossiness with Rolf and John. I'm surprised he even considered letting Mark interfere with the delicate project of the labyrinth, but perhaps he was testing him.

"We already have enough help," I say. "Suchart usually cooks with us. Maybe you can find a cleaning task. The bathroom is pretty dirty."

Mark glares at me.

"We've found that too many cooks spoil the soup," I continue, "or whatever the saying is." I try to lighten the mood with a joke. "That's why Rolf and John are never in here. They're banned because they've scorched every pot of lentils they've ever tried to cook." This is actually true—Rolf and John's cooking is an abomination.

"Well, Somchai wants me here," Mark says, opening another cupboard and rifling through it. "Let's compromise." His back is turned to me. "How about we make my stew today, and your stir-fry tomorrow?"

In the end, Tep and I let Mark have his way. It seems like the easiest solution. But I am furious. The next morning, after sweeping the hall, I go to find Som.

It's a cold day but he's sitting out on the small patch of grass in front of the hall with his shirt and pant legs rolled up, catching the weak October rays. On his lap is an open book. He has recently taken up reading literature and can often be found pouring over a novel in the afternoon.

He smiles as he sees me approach. Looking at my face, he holds up a hand. "No," he says.

"What?" I stop a few paces in front of him.

"I don't accept."

"What?"

"You are coming to me with a gift. A gift of your anger. And I don't accept it." He turns back to his book and, using his finger to underline the words, continues to read.

I stare at him, not sure what to say.

He scratches his nose and turns a page. Several uncomfortable moments pass—uncomfortable for me, that is. Som seems perfectly at ease. Finally, he looks up at me. "Do you have another gift?"

I don't have anything, not even a bar of the expensive fair trade chocolate I usually bring him when I come back from visiting the city.

"Nothing?" His face is amused.

"A joke?" I finally venture. I can't think of any, but hope one might come to me.

Som smiles. "Okay." He holds up his book. "Look." The cover reads *Japanese Death Poems*. He recites: "A turtle dried its shell out/in the first sun rays of the year." He laughs. "It's like me. A dry old turtle in the sun." He laughs again.

I smile in spite of myself, realizing as I do that my anger has dissolved like a cloud of fog blown off the top of a mountain.

Som sets the book down open-faced on his lap and looks up at me. His brown eyes are kind. "Mark needs to learn. You work with him, you help me. I ask for your help."

Part of me wants to argue with him, but the same wind that blew away my anger has also blown away much of my desire to fight. I know the annoyance will resurface, but in this moment, I feel resigned. "Okay," I say. "But Tep and I still get to choose the menu. Will you tell him that?"

Som smiles. "As you wish. It is good for him to follow directions."

After a couple of weeks, Mark quits coming to the kitchen. He seems to have lost his interest in cooking since he can't call the shots. But it isn't long before I discover that he has taken up a new project.

I arrive early to tea one evening and, walking down the hall, hear him talking in the kitchen.

"This place needs help. Have you seen the pantry? There's barely anything there. What are we going to eat?"

I stop to listen, and hear Rolf reply. "Yeah, Suchart told me the food is low."

"And there's no money to get more. We need to do something."

It's true the place is in financial trouble. Some months ago, at Som's request, John cut the prayer flags from the wooden sign and painted "Kanda Spiritual Centre" in dark red letters over "Kanda Monastery." Once the monastery became a centre, many of the already lax rules were further relaxed. Once word of Som's highly unorthodox ways got out, the former supporters—many of them devout followers of the Theravada tradition, some wealthy, most living in the city—ceased to visit with gifts of food and money. We've been living on the centre's savings, food from the garden, and stores from previous years. We are down to our last two bags of rice and our last canister of beans.

I don't hear Rolf reply, but I hear the sound of the kettle being slammed down on the stove and the hiss of the gas. I enter the kitchen to see Rolf sitting with his chin in his hands, looking down at the table. Mark is busying himself at the stove, making a pot of green tea.

"We have to get some money," he is saying. "Or we won't eat. You don't want to starve, do you?"

Rolf looks up at me with an inscrutable expression. Before he can say anything, Tep and Suchart walk in. Suchart sits down and Tep goes to the pantry and comes back empty-handed. There hasn't been any chocolate for weeks, but somehow we all keep forgetting this. Mark brings the pot and a few cups to the table. His black eyes flick over us. John is absent—probably meditating on his own, as he does some evenings. We sit in uneasy stillness, until Suchart picks up the pot and pours us each a cup of tea.

We are sipping our tea when Som walks in. His appearance is unexpected, as he usually leaves us to ourselves at tea time. He gets himself a cup from the cupboard and comes to sit down, lifting the pot to pour himself some tea. Only a few drops plop into his cup. He sets down the pot and looks around the table at each of us. Tep jumps up to boil more water, but Som motions for him to sit down. There is a heavy silence, and underneath it I feel Mark's flickering energy from across the table.

Finally Som speaks. "My mother," he says.

I have been staring at my tea but look up now and accidentally catch Rolf's eyes. He looks distracted. Mark stares down at his teacup while Suchart looks out the window. Only Tep and I seem to be focussed on Som.

"Her picture is gone. Has anyone seen it?" Som asks.

No one answers. Water drips from the kitchen faucet and the stove creaks as it cools. I feel something radiating, cold—is it Mark's energy, or the general unease? Why doesn't anyone speak?

"Well," Som finally says, "if you find it, please give it back. I miss her." He lifts his cup to his mouth and tilts it back, but then remembers there is nothing in it and sets it back down. He lifts himself from the stool and walks slowly out of the kitchen.

Exiting my hut the next day, I see Rolf and Mark talking intensely with John beside the labyrinth. They are in a sort of huddle. It's raining, but only Mark's head is covered by the hood of a rain jacket. John and Rolf are in their tattered, wet robes. I decide to creep into the woods and back around behind them to see if I can get close enough to hear anything.

Crouching behind a tree, I hear Mark explaining. "It will just be a simple place where people can stop by for a cup of tea. Like a cafe. But spiritual. A spiritual cafe. We can sell a few things. Prayer flags, pottery. I have a connection who can get us cheap stuff from Cambodia."

"I don't know…" John's voice is uncertain. "I'm not sure Som will like it."

"If we leave this all in Somchai's hands, the centre won't last more than a few weeks. We're almost out of food. And there's no savings."

"There's savings," Rolf says. "There's some. I'm not sure exactly how much. But I think enough to last awhile."

"How do you know?" Mark challenges. "It's all hearsay. I wouldn't be surprised if we're already looking at a zero balance."

I've noticed that Mark has been using the word "we" a lot lately when he talks about the centre, even though he's only been here a couple of weeks. Shielded by the tree, I can't see his face, but I imagine him smiling that weird smile of his, the one that never reaches his eyes.

There's this shiftiness to Mark; it always feels like he is partially somewhere else. Often, while walking in the woods or sweeping the hall, I think I see him out of the corner of my eye—but when I turn he's not there. Often I have the sense that he might just dissolve as I'm talking to him. There is something shadowy about him, even when he is standing in bright sunlight.

A large raindrop breaks through the boughs and lands on my forehead, running down my nose. I want to run also, back to my hut, back to my meditation, but I am here now and have to keep listening.

"Maybe we should talk to Som about it tonight," John offers.

"I think he might be more receptive to our idea if everything is in place. I can get down to the city today and see my friend about the space. She owes me—so she'll give us a loan for the first two months. One of you should come with me. Rolf?"

I don't hear Rolf answer, but I imagine him shrugging, which means he'll go along with Mark's plan, even if he doesn't think it is a good idea.

"Or John? Maybe John would be better," Mark says. "John is more of a people person, better at these sorts of things. If you don't mind, Rolf."

"I don't care," says Rolf. "I didn't want to go anyway."

"Well, good then—it's settled. Now who will tell Somchai?"

"Don't you think it's best that you tell him?" asks John.

"Maybe," says Mark. "I mean, it is my idea. But you two have known him longer. He's more comfortable with you. He trusts you."

Mark usually avoids me, so I'm surprised when he shows up in the kitchen a few days later as I'm washing dishes. A cold wind sweeps in with him. As usual, he is bundled up in layers of clothing. He has stopped wearing his sunglasses inside, but he still blinks constantly.

"Cold, Mark?" I attempt a teasing tone.

He grimaces in response and stalks to the stove, putting on the teakettle. "I thought I'd bring some tea to Somchai."

Just as he says this, Som walks in. "You wanted to talk?"

"Yes." Mark blinks rapidly. "I was just making you some tea. But...I was hoping we could go to your office. It's a delicate matter." He glances at me.

"We can talk here," Som says, pulling a stool up to the big wooden table. "Misaki, you don't mind, do you?"

I shake my head, turning back to the sink to squeeze more soap onto the bowls.

"So," says Som.

"I wanted to talk to you about something important," says Mark. "A sort of…venture. John and Rolf and I have been talking. We thought it might be nice…helpful to open a tea shop in the city."

Som doesn't reply.

Mark continues, "It would be both a gathering place, a place where people can come together to meet, to talk, but also a place to raise money for the centre." He pauses. "We noticed that the centre seems to be…struggling."

"How is the centre struggling?" Som asks.

Mark doesn't answer, but ploughs on. "We also thought we could sell things at the shop. Spiritual things—singing bowls, tapestries, incense. Maybe even some books. And I thought you might be interested in sharing some of your sayings. We could paint them on prayer flags or have an artist use calligraphy on some high quality rice paper, frame them in bamboo—we could easily sell them for a hundred bucks."

At this, Som laughs. "Sell sayings?"

I am tempted to turn from the sink so I can see Mark's face, but I don't want to draw attention to myself.

"'You are the peace you are seeking,'" Mark intones. "Remember that one?"

Som laughs. "Not mine."

"Love all, serve all."

Som laughs again. "Where did you get this?"

Mark doesn't reply, but I imagine him looking blankly at Som with those flat black eyes of his.

Som's voice is suddenly serious. "No. We won't sell."

"But if the centre is going to stay open, we need money." Mark's tone is curt. "What are we going to do? We could charge visitors to walk around the labyrinth, if those two idiots would ever finish it."

"Enough!" Som's voice is louder than I have ever heard it. There is a long pause. The temperature seems to drop several degrees. I slowly scrub the same fork I have been washing for several minutes.

Som finally speaks. "Who trained you?" he asks gently.

"What do you mean?" Mark's voice is noncommittal.

"Who taught you? All this money stuff?"

"Taught me?"

"Okay." Som sounds resigned. "You don't have to say. But nothing will be sold here. Not at the centre. Open this shop if you wish."

Mark gives a sort of hissing sigh. But when he speaks, his voice is polite. "Thank you, Somchai. I promise we won't disappoint you. And we will get funds for the centre, to make it better than ever. People will start coming again. You'll see."

"I don't care about this," Som replies. "People come when they come. But go ahead. Open your shop." With this, he gets up and shuffles out of the room.

My back is still turned to Mark, which always makes me slightly nervous. I listen for his retreat, but don't hear anything. Suddenly he is right beside me, looking at my face. The dry patch on his forehead has grown; it's peeling, an irritated red. His black eyes blink rapidly. I can't read anything in them.

"It's for the best," he says.

"What is?" I try to keep my voice calm.

"Everything. The shop. Somchai will see that soon enough. And so will you." His smile is a dry crack opening his face. He moves as if to touch my shoulder, then drops his hand abruptly. I look down at the fork in my hand, afraid to look in his eyes again. When I look up, he's gone.

Weeks pass. I don't see Mark much. He spends most of his time in the city, getting the tea shop up and running. John and Rolf usually accompany him. Sometimes Mark is dropped off by a black Mercedes driven by a glossy-haired woman in a business suit who honks and waves at us before spinning the car around and racing back down the mountain.

When the three of them are gone, the centre feels peaceful again. In the mornings, Tep and I cook together. Som gave Suchart money to buy more supplies, and the pantry is full of dried peppers and herbs, ropes of garlic, beans and grains. In the afternoons, Tep teaches me songs in Pali and Suchart works on his sewing. He has taken to altering the garments we pick up from free boxes and thrift stores in the city, letting out the dresses and blouses that Tep favours and hemming Som's jeans and button-up shirts to the right length.

Mark, John, and Rolf are gone so often that I grow accustomed to seeing three empty mats in the meditation hall, but one evening I arrive to see everyone sitting in their usual places, eyes closed, already meditating. I slip to the back and take my seat. We wait in silence for Som, who shuffles in after a few minutes. "Today we will start with the discourse," he says, "and med-itate after."

"When she got old, my mother had a beard," he begins. "Like this." He tugs at the few tufts of hair sprouting from his chin. "But nicer." He runs his finger over the slight moustache bristling above his lip. "And this. A small one. Very nice."

He tells us that once, when she was a girl walking on her way to school, she saw a dragon climb out of a muddy, rain-swollen river. "It didn't hurt her," he says. "It was friendly. It wanted to know her name. It didn't give her any wishes, like a fairytale." He laughs. "It didn't turn into a prince and marry her. It was just curious. That was the only time she saw it."

Som pauses for a long time. I am wondering about the import of the story when he continues. "My mother . . . at the monastery, after the silence vow, she wrote on a board with chalk. And that is how she told me about a calling. A calling . . . some of you un-derstand. Some of you have this. And some of you . . . "

He looks around the room at us. His face looks tired and sad. I glance down at my hands in my lap, wishing I could help him.

"I am disappointed, very disappointed," he says quietly. "The picture is still gone. Maybe it is lost. But I don't think so." He looks carefully at the floor and then at the windows. It's only just after six, but the winter darkness presses against glass. The low lamps normally give the hall a warm feel, but this evening the room is unusually cold. Even though I am wearing a scarf and a sweater, I find myself shivering.

Som shakes his head. "No one has returned it."

I hear someone shift on their cushion uneasily.

"You worry about money," Som starts slowly. "You worry will the centre be okay. Okay. If you have questions about this stuff, you ask. But do not steal. Never steal."

He seems to be waiting for a response from someone, but no one says anything. "Let us meditate," he finally says. I am relieved to close my eyes and enter the darkness.

Som calls me to his office the next day to ask me to run some errands in the city. He wants me to drop a book off to a former devotee and pick up some tea from the tea shop. He hasn't been to the tea shop yet, and neither have I. I am both nervous and curious to see it. Mark has said it's doing well, but he hasn't encouraged us to visit. "In a few weeks," he keeps saying, "once we're established."

I catch the early bus and get to the city before noon. It is the same as always, cold and rainy, full of people cowering under umbrellas and rushing into buildings, never meeting one another's eyes. The tea shop is in a quieter neighbourhood, a few blocks off Main Street, in the first floor of an old, turquoise house with yellow trim. Two people are sitting on the front porch drinking from small ceramic cups. A string of prayer flags decorates the doorway. Above it, in careful black calligraphy, are the words "Mother's Tea Shop."

I hesitate on the sidewalk. Why has Mark named it this? Who is Mother? And what if Mark is inside, and no one else? What if I'm alone with him?

I gather my courage and walk up the steps. The two people continue their quiet conversation and do not look at me.

Inside, the tea shop is large, painted a bright orange, with a few couches and low tables. There are shelves laden with spiritual memorabilia, tapestries and prints on the walls. Near the window, a large table bearing a "sale" sign is covered with miniature stone labyrinths. Next to it, a white woman in a flowing, printed dress is examining a small object in her hands as Mark leans over her.

"That's Mother, the patron saint of our shop," Mark is explaining. "I can't sell you it, because it's an original, the only one we have. But we're having framed replicas made in our workshop, and I could have one ready for you next week."

The woman murmurs something in a grateful tone, and Mark looks up at me.

But it's not Mark.

The face is green, scaly—the face of a reptile. Its red tongue darts out, then retreats. The eyes are the only feature I recognize, flat and black.

My heart jolts in my chest. I am too stunned to speak. The hair rises on my arms, at the back of my neck.

Before I can do anything, the face morphs into Mark's. His eyes look angry, but this look is quickly swallowed up by a blankness. "Misaki," he says evenly. "This is a surprise."

It's difficult to speak. Nausea churns in the pit of my stomach. I am thankful we're not alone. My whole body feels cold. Although I am shivering, I manage to sound calm when I say, "Som wanted me to pick up some tea."

"I see." He blinks rapidly.

The woman next to him looks up at me, smiling. "This place

is so special," she says. "I've never been to a cafe with a patron saint. *And* it sells art." She waves an arm around the room. She is still holding the small object, which I see now is a picture.

I take a step closer. "Can I see that? I ask.

"Sure." She is about to give it to me when Mark snatches it out of her hand.

"This is very precious," he says. "Invaluable. One of a kind. That's why we usually don't let customers touch it, although you are a rare exception." He attempts to smile charmingly at the woman, but the smile twists his face in a strange way, as if it might pull it in two. I'm afraid I might see the lizard again and so I look quickly at the floor. When I look up, Mark is stalking over to the register. Before I can say anything, he slips the picture in a drawer.

The woman looks confused. "I guess you won't hang it over the door anymore, then," she says wistfully. "But at least I'll have my own next week."

Mark's head is down as he appears to be calculating something on a piece of paper. I know I'd better move quickly or I'll be left alone with him. I pick up a bag of green tea from one of the shelves. "Please put this on the centre's account," I say, walking to the door. The woman is admiring some hand-woven bags.

Mark doesn't look up from the register. "See you at the centre," he says.

I have never been more anxious to leave the city—but the bus is late, the trail slippery with mud. Bushes crowd onto the path and grab at my clothes. It seems I will never get to the top of the mountain. Finally I round the corner and see the clearing, the familiar shape of the meditation hall. I all but run to Som's office, but when I knock, he doesn't answer. I hear someone behind me and turn.

It's John. It seems ridiculous to be afraid, but a thrill of fear runs through me. Has Mark sent him? Since he's been working in the tea shop, John has started wearing layperson's clothes. I think I recognize his tie-dyed shirt from a rack in the tea shop.

"Back from the shop?" I ask, not mentioning that I have just come from there.

John shakes his head. "I'm done with that place."

"Oh?"

"It's...weird. I'd rather be up here."

"What about Rolf?" I ask.

"I don't know," he says. "He's still making stuff to sell at the shop."

I pause, considering this. I want to ask him about the picture, but think better of it. "Have you seen Som?"

"Not today. I was just coming to see if I could meet with him."

"Me too."

Just then Som walks up. He is carrying a box of expensive chocolates from a chocolatier in the city. "Look what my old student gave us," he says, beaming. "Five months he does not visit— then this." He takes the lid off the box. "Here, have one." I grab one with caramel and pecans and John lingers over the box before finally deciding on a white chocolate truffle. We chew as Som smiles at us.

"John, the labyrinth looks good. I'm glad you've returned."

John looks bashful. He shrugs, smiling down at the floor.

"Misaki, I can meet with you. It's okay, John?"

"No problem," John says. "We can meet later. I have some rocks to collect."

John walks off as Som opens the door of his office, carefully balancing the chocolates in one hand. He sets the box on the desk and pops one in his mouth before sitting down on his mat. I have already taken the mat facing his. He chews his chocolate, looking at the floor. Finally, he swallows it, and looks up at me.

"Well?"

"I got the tea," I say.

He smiles. "You came to tell me this?"

"No." I feel as nervous as I did the first time I sat across from him. How to begin? I clear my throat. "I think I know what happened to the picture of your mother," I say.

He looks at me without saying anything. His face is serene.

"It's at the tea shop."

Som considers this. He licks his teeth, clearing them of the final bits of chocolate, before replying. "Are you sure?"

I hesitate. "I'm pretty sure."

"Did you see it?"

"Not close up," I have to admit. "But from what I could tell, it was the picture of your mother. And Mark was acting very strange about it. Very strange. He hid it away and wouldn't let me see it."

"Hid it away?"

"He put it in a drawer."

"You didn't see it?"

"No," I say, feeling stupid. What if I'm wrong?

Som shrugs. "It doesn't matter. If it was the picture or not. So he took it." Unexpectedly, he laughs. "Actually, I love that picture too much. Maybe that's why he took it." He shakes his head, still smiling. "I never wanted anyone to take it. I loved it too much." He lapses into silence, a small smile on his face.

I imagine Som's mother's happy face, the bamboo towering above her. I have seen the photo so many times that it takes no effort to conjure it in my mind. The same must be true for Som.

But I have to tell him Mark's plan. "He's going to reproduce it—sell copies in the shop."

When I say this, Som's expression turns serious. He nods thoughtfully. "Yes. I guess that could happen."

"There's something else I have to tell you." As I say this, my nervousness returns— rivulets of anxious energy run through my body. I can't look at his face.

"Yes?" Som seems to be coming back from somewhere deep in his mind.

"At the tea shop," I begin. "At the tea shop...I saw Mark."

"And?"

"He wasn't Mark."

"Who was he?"

"A lizard."

Som laughs and slaps his leg. He gets up to grab the box of chocolates from the desk and brings it over, offering me one. I am so surprised by Som's response that I take two instead, shoving a truffle in my mouth and devouring it in one bite. Som sits down, gnawing a hunk of peanut brittle. "Yes," he says, chewing. "I know this."

"You knew?"

"Yes." He swallows the peanut brittle and contemplates the box of chocolates.

"How long did you know?"

"From the start. I saw him sleeping one time."

"Why did you let him stay?" I am incredulous.

Som shrugs. "He wanted to."

"But—"

"So he is hiding," Som interrupts. "So? You too were hiding when you came here." He examines the chocolates as if one might contain a secret message. Then he sighs and puts the lid on the box, pushing it aside. He looks at me intently. "Good, bad..." He waves his hand in the air as if dispelling some insignificant idea. "Mark might learn. Still he might learn. And if he doesn't..." His words trail away as he looks at the lamp lit on the desk behind me. Then he closes his eyes. Again he seems far off, somewhere deep in his own mind.

Finally he opens his eyes. "He is like any of us," he concludes. "Except a lizard. Okay?"

"He is not like me!" I am suddenly angry. "What if he turns on us? What if he comes while we're sleeping?"

Som laughs. Then he looks at me tenderly. "Misaki. Misaki. Don't worry. He can't hurt you. Soon, he will get bored, and leave. If there's nothing to feed him, he won't stay."

"But what about the shop?"

Som shrugs. "Let him keep it."

I suddenly have an image of Mark in the tea shop, an angry look contorting his patchy face. He sweeps his arm across the table of miniature labyrinths and the labyrinths crash to the floor.

Then I see him as a lizard, trapped in the centre of an ancient stone labyrinth. He darts down a path, hits a dead end. Turns, runs—another dead end. He bumps a hard wall, turns again—and then he is spinning around and around, chasing his own tail.

I am floating above the labyrinth. From a great height, I see weeds sprouting in stone cracks, pebbles on the dusty paths. The labyrinth appears to be empty, but I know there is something there because I am looking for it.

I hear Som's voice. "When you find it."

"What?" I ask. And as I watch, the labyrinth starts slowly turning—then it picks up speed—chunks of stone and clumps of weed fall away—it's spinning rapidly, a grey-green blur—

And in the swirling, all I can hear is Som's laughter.

ACKNOWLEDGEMENTS

This book was written on the unceded ancestral territories of the Musqueam, Squamish, Tsleil-Waututh, and Qayqayt peoples.

Many thanks to my editors Jennifer Chapis and Hiromi Goto, and my publishers, Brian Kaufman and Karen Green, for their helpful suggestions. Thanks also to Cara Lang at Anvil Press for all her help.

Deep bows to my first readers, who gave invaluable feedback on early drafts of nearly every one of these stories: Christine Leclerc and Karen Smith.

Thank you also to my other readers who gave suggestions on one or more of these stories: Thea Bowering, Mercedes Eng, Monica Hepburn, Brook Houglum, Kim Minkus, Jordan Scott, and Cathy Stonehouse.

Three wonderful writers were kind enough to take time out of their busy schedules to read this book and provide blurbs. Big gratitude to Kevin Chong, Wayde Compton, and Shaena Lambert.

Thank you to Kwantlen Polytechnic University's .06% PD Fund, which gave me much-needed time to work on this book.

Thanks to the editors and readers of the following publications in which these stories first appeared, sometimes in different versions and with different titles: *Broken Pencil, Canthius, The Capilano Review, Duende, The Nashwaak Review, Plentitude, PRISM International, Room,* and *The Windsor Review.*

Lastly, so much gratitude to my partner Karen and my beloved friends and family for their love and support. Without you, these stories wouldn't exist.

ABOUT THE AUTHOR

Jen Currin lives on the unceded land of the Qayqayt peoples (New Westminster, BC) and has published four collections of poetry, including *The Inquisition Yours*, which won the 2011 Audre Lorde Award for Lesbian Poetry; and *School* (2014), which was a finalist for three awards. Jen's poems and stories have been published in many journals and anthologies. An instructor of creative writing at Kwantlen Polytechnic University, Jen also teaches community workshops and grows vegetables in her community garden plot.

AUTHOR PHOTO: SARAH RACE PHOTOGRAPHY